Kim Kostal
NAME

THE GRIM GROTTO

✳ A Series of Unfortunate Events ✳

BOOK the Eleventh

THE GRIM GROTTO

by LEMONY SNICKET

Illustrations by Brett Helquist

■ HarperCollinsPublishers

www.harperchildrens.com

Library of Congress Cataloging-in-Publication Data is available.

ISBN 0-06-441014-5—ISBN 0-06-029642-9 (lib. bdg.)

1   3   5   7   9   10   8   6   4   2
❖
First Edition

For Beatrice—
Dead women tell no tales.
Sad men write them down.

THE GRIM GROTTO

CHAPTER

One

After a great deal of time examining oceans, investigating rainstorms, and staring very hard at several drinking fountains, the scientists of the world developed a theory regarding how water is distributed around our planet, which they have named "the water cycle." The water cycle consists of three key phenomena—evaporation, precipitation, and collection—and all of them are equally boring.

Of course, it is boring to read about boring things, but it is better to read something that makes you yawn with boredom than something that will make you weep uncontrollably, pound your fists against the floor, and leave tearstains all over your pillowcase, sheets, and boomerang collection. Like the water cycle, the tale of the Baudelaire children consists of three key phenomena, but rather than read their sorry tale it would be best if you read something about the water cycle instead.

Violet, the eldest phenomenon, was nearly fifteen years old and very nearly the best inventor the world had ever seen. As far as I can tell she was certainly the best inventor who had ever found herself trapped in the gray waters of the Stricken Stream, clinging desperately to a toboggan as she was carried away from the Valley of Four Drafts, and if I were you I would prefer to focus on the boring phenomenon of evaporation, which refers to the process of water turning into vapor and eventually forming clouds, rather than think about the turmoil that awaited her at the bottom of the Mortmain Mountains.

Klaus was the second eldest of the Baudelaire siblings, but it would be better for your

health if you concentrated on the boring phenomenon of precipitation, which refers to vapor
turning back into water and falling as rain, rather
than spending even one moment thinking about
the phenomenon of Klaus's excellent skills as a
researcher, and the amount of trouble and woe
these skills would bring him once he and his siblings met up with Count Olaf, the notorious villain who had been after the children ever since
their parents had perished in a terrible fire.

And even Sunny Baudelaire, who had
recently passed out of babyhood, is a phenomenon all to herself, not only for her very sharp
teeth, which had helped the Baudelaires in a
number of unpleasant circumstances, but also
for her newfound skills as a cook, which had fed
the Baudelaires in a number of unpleasant circumstances. Although the phenomenon of collection, which describes the gathering of fallen
rain into one place so it can evaporate once more
and begin the entire tedious process all over
again, is probably the most boring phenomenon

in the water cycle, it would be far better for you to get up and go right to your nearest library and spend several boring days reading every single boring fact you can find about collection, because the phenomenon of what happens to Sunny Baudelaire over the course of these pages is the most dreadful phenomenon I can think of, and I can think of a great many. The water cycle may be a series of boring phenomena, but the story of the Baudelaires is something else entirely, and this is an excellent opportunity to read something boring instead of learning what became of the Baudelaires as the rushing waters of the Stricken Stream carried them away from the mountains.

"What will become of us?" Violet asked, raising her voice to be heard over the rushing water. "I don't think I can invent anything that can stop this toboggan."

"I don't think you should try," Klaus called back to his sister. "The arrival of False Spring has thawed out the stream, but the waters are still very cold. If one of us fell into the stream, I'm not sure how long we could survive."

"Quigley," Sunny whimpered. The youngest Baudelaire often talked in a way that could be difficult to understand, but lately her speech had been developing almost as quickly as her cooking skills, and her siblings knew that Sunny was referring to Quigley Quagmire, with whom the Baudelaires had recently become friends. Quigley had helped Violet and Klaus reach the top of Mount Fraught in order to find the V.F.D. headquarters and rescue Sunny from Count Olaf's clutches, but another tributary of the Stricken Stream had carried him off in the opposite direction, and the cartographer—a word which here means "someone who is very good with maps, and of whom Violet Baudelaire was particularly fond"—didn't even have a toboggan to keep him out of the chilly water.

"I'm sure Quigley has gotten out of the water," Violet said quickly, although of course she was sure of no such thing. "I only wish we knew where he was going. He told us to meet him somewhere, but the waterfall interrupted him."

The toboggan bobbed in the water as Klaus reached into his pocket and drew out a dark blue notebook. The notebook had been a gift from Quigley, and Klaus was using it as a commonplace book, a phrase which here means "notebook in which he wrote any interesting or useful information." "We decoded that message telling us about an important V.F.D. gathering on Thursday," he said, "and thanks to Sunny, we know that the meeting is at the Hotel Denouement. Maybe that's where Quigley wants to meet us—at the last safe place."

"But we don't know where it is," Violet pointed out. "How can we meet someone in an unknown location?"

The three Baudelaires sighed, and for a few moments the siblings sat quietly on the toboggan and listened to the gurgling of the stream. There are some people who like to watch a stream for hours, staring at the glittering water and thinking about the mysteries of the world. But the waters of the Stricken Stream were too dirty to glitter, and every mystery the children tried to solve seemed to reveal even more mysteries, and even those mysteries contained mysteries, so when they pondered these mysteries they felt more overwhelmed than thoughtful. They knew that V.F.D. was a secret organization, but they couldn't seem to find out much about what the organization did, or why it should concern the Baudelaires. They knew that Count Olaf was very eager to get his filthy hands on a certain sugar bowl, but they had no idea why the sugar bowl was so important, or where in the world it was. They knew that there were people in the world who could help them, but so many of these people—guardians, friends, bankers—had proven to be of no help at all, or had vanished from their lives just when the Baudelaires needed them most. And they knew there were people in the world who would not help them—villainous people, and their number seemed to be growing as their treachery and wickedness trickled all over the earth, like a dreadful water cycle of woe and despair. But right now the biggest mystery seemed to be what to do next, and as the Baudelaires huddled together on the floating toboggan they could not think of a thing.

"If we stay on the toboggan," Violet said finally, "where do you think we'll go?"

"Down the mountains," Klaus said. "Water runs downhill. The Stricken Stream probably leads out of the Mortmain Mountains into the hinterlands, and then eventually it'll lead to some larger body of water—a lake, or an ocean. From there the water will evaporate into clouds, fall as rain and snow, and so on."

"Tedium," Sunny said.

"The water cycle is quite dull," Klaus agreed, "but it might be the easiest way to get us away from Count Olaf."

"That's true," Violet said. "Olaf said he'd be right behind us."

"Esmelita," Sunny said, which meant something like, "Along with Esmé Squalor and Carmelita Spats," and the Baudelaires frowned as they thought of Olaf's girlfriend, who participated in Olaf's schemes because she believed that treachery and deception were very stylish, or "in," and the former classmate of the Baudelaires' who had recently joined Olaf for selfish reasons of her own.

"So we're just going to sit on this toboggan," Violet asked, "and see where it takes us?"

"It's not much of a plan," Klaus admitted, "but I can't think of a better one."

"Passive," Sunny said, and her siblings nodded glumly. "Passive" is an unusual word to hear from a baby, and in fact it is an unusual word to hear from a Baudelaire or anyone else who leads an interesting life. It merely means "accepting what is happening without doing anything about it," and certainly everyone has passive moments from time to time. Perhaps you have experienced a passive moment at the shoe store, when you sat in a chair as the shoe salesperson forced your feet into a series of ugly and uncomfortable shoes, when all the while you wanted a bright red pair with strange buckles that nobody on earth was going to buy for you. The Baudelaires had experienced a passive moment at Briny Beach, where they had learned the terrible news about their parents, and had been numbly led by Mr. Poe toward their new unfortunate lives. I recently experienced a passive moment myself, sitting in a chair as a shoe salesperson forced my feet into a series of ugly and uncomfortable positions, when all the while I wanted a bright red pair of shoes with strange buckles that nobody on earth was going to buy for me. But a passive moment in the middle of a rushing stream, when villainous people are hot on your trail, is a difficult moment to accept, which is why the Baudelaires fidgeted on the toboggan as the Stricken Stream carried them further and further downhill, just as I fidgeted as I tried to plan my escape from that sinister shoe emporium. Violet fidgeted and thought of Quigley, hoping he had managed to escape from the cold water and get himself to safety. Klaus fidgeted and thought of V.F.D., hoping that he could still learn more about the organization even though their headquarters had been destroyed. And Sunny fidgeted and thought of the fish in the Stricken Stream, who would occasionally stick their heads out of the ashen water and cough. She was wondering if the ashes, which were left in the water by a recent fire in the mountains and made it difficult for the fish to breathe, would mean the fish wouldn't taste very good, even if you used a recipe with plenty of butter and lemon.

The Baudelaires were so busy fidgeting and thinking that when the toboggan rounded one of the odd, square sides of the mountain peaks, it was a moment before they noticed the view spread below them. Only when a few scraps of newspaper blew in front of their faces did the Baudelaires look down and gasp at what they saw.

"What is it?" Violet said.

"I don't know," Klaus said. "It's hard to tell from so high up."

"Subjavik," Sunny said, and she spoke the truth. From this side of the Mortmain Mountains, the Baudelaires had expected to see the hinterlands, a vast expanse of flat landscape where they had spent quite some time. Instead, it looked like the world had turned into a dark, dark sea. As far as the eye could see there were swirls of gray and black, moving like strange eels in shadowy water. Every so often one of the swirls would release a small, fragile object that would float up toward the Baudelaires like a feather. Some of these objects were scraps of newspaper. Others appeared to be tiny bits of cloth. And some of them were so dark that they were utterly unrecognizable, a phrase Sunny preferred to express as "subjavik."

Klaus squinted down through his glasses and then turned to his sisters with a look of despair.

"I know what it is," he said quietly. "It's the ruins of a fire."

The Baudelaires looked down again and saw that Klaus was right. From such a height, it had taken the children a moment to realize that a great fire had raged through the hinterlands, leaving only ashen scraps behind.

"Of course," Violet said. "It's strange we didn't recognize it before. But who would set fire to the hinterlands?"

"We did," Klaus said.

"Caligari," Sunny said, reminding Violet of a terrible carnival in which the Baudelaires had spent some time in disguise. Sadly, as part of their disguise it had been necessary to assist Count Olaf in burning down the carnival, and now they could see the fruits of their labors, a phrase which here means "the results of the terrible thing they did, even though they did not mean to do it at all."

"The fire isn't our fault," Violet said. "Not entirely. We *had* to help Olaf, otherwise he would have discovered our disguises."

"He discovered our disguises anyway," Klaus pointed out.

"Noblaym," Sunny said, which meant something like, "But it's still not our fault."

"Sunny's right," Violet said. "We didn't think up the plot—Olaf did."

"We didn't stop him, either," Klaus pointed out. "And plenty of people think we're entirely responsible. These scraps of newspaper are probably from *The Daily Punctilio*, which has blamed us for all sorts of terrible crimes."

"You're right," Violet said with a sigh, although I have since discovered that Klaus was wrong, and that the scraps of paper blowing past the Baudelaires were from another publication that would have been of enormous help had they stopped to collect the pieces. "Maybe we should be passive for a while. Being active hasn't helped us much."

"In any case," Klaus said, "we should stay

on the toboggan. Fire can't hurt us if we're float-ing on a stream."

"It doesn't seem like we have a choice," Violet said. "Look."

The Baudelaires looked, and saw that the toboggan was approaching a sort of intersection, where another tributary of the Stricken Stream was meeting up with theirs. The stream was now much wider, and the water even rougher, so the Baudelaires had to hang on tight in order not to be thrown into the deepening waters.

"We must be approaching a larger body of water," Klaus said. "We're further along in the water cycle than I thought."

"Do you think that's the tributary that car-ried away Quigley?" Violet said, craning her neck to look for her missing friend.

"Selphawa!" Sunny cried, which meant "We can't think about Quigley now—we have to think about ourselves," and the youngest Bau-delaire was right. With a great *whoosh!* the stream turned another square corner, and within moments the waters of the stream were churning so violently that it felt as if the Baudelaires were riding a wild horse rather than a broken toboggan.

"Can you steer the toboggan toward the shore?" Klaus yelled over the sound of the stream.

"No!" Violet cried. "The steering mechanism broke when we rode down the waterfall, and the stream is too wide to paddle there!" Violet found a ribbon in her pocket and paused to tie up her hair in order to think better. She gazed down at the toboggan and tried to think of various mechanical blueprints she had read in her childhood, when her parents were alive and supportive of her interests in mechanical engineering. "The runners of the toboggan," she said, and then repeated it in a shout to be heard over the water. "The runners! They help the toboggan maneuver on the snow, but maybe they can help us steer on the water!"

"Where are the runners?" Klaus asked, looking around.

"On the bottom of the toboggan!" Violet cried.

"Imposiyakto?" Sunny asked, which meant something like, "How can we get to the bottom of the toboggan?"

"I don't know," Violet said, and frantically checked her pockets for any inventing materials. She had been carrying a long bread knife, but now it was gone—probably carried away by the stream, along with Quigley, when she had used it last. She looked straight ahead, at the frothy rush of water threatening to engulf them. She gazed at the distant shores of the stream, which grew more and more distant as the stream continued to widen. And she looked at her siblings, who were waiting for her inventing skills to save them. Her siblings looked back, and all three Baudelaires looked at one another for a moment, blinking dark water out of their eyes, as they tried to think of something to do.

Just at that moment, however, one more eye arrived, also blinking dark water as it rose out of the stream, right in front of the Baudelaires. At first it seemed to be the eye of some terrible sea creature, found only in books of mythology and in the swimming pools of certain resorts. But as the toboggan took them closer, the children could see that the eye was made of metal, perched on top of a long metal pole that curved at the top so the eye could get a better look at them. It is very unusual to see a metal eye rising up out of the rushing waters of a stream, and yet this eye was something the Baudelaires had seen many times, since their first encounter with an eye tattoo on Count Olaf's left ankle. The eye was an insignia, and when you looked at it in a certain way it also looked like three mysterious letters.

"V.F.D.!" Sunny cried, as the toboggan drew even closer.

"What is it?" Klaus asked.

"It's a periscope!" Violet said. "Submarines

use them to look at things above the water!"

"Does that mean," Klaus cried, "that there's a submarine beneath us?"

Violet did not have to answer, because the eye rose further out of the water, and the orphans could see that the pole was attached to a large, flat piece of metal, most of which was under the water. The toboggan drew closer until the periscope was in reach, and then stopped, the way a raft will stop when it hits a large rock.

"Look!" Violet cried as the stream rushed around them. She pointed to a hatch just at the bottom of the periscope. "Let's knock—maybe they can hear us!"

"But we have no idea who's inside," Klaus said.

"Taykashans!" Sunny shrieked, which meant "It's our only chance to travel safely through these waters," and she leaned down to the hatch and scraped at it with her teeth. Her siblings joined her, preferring to use their fists to pound on the metal hatch.

"Hello!" Violet cried.

"Hello!" Klaus yelled.

"Shalom!" Sunny shrieked.

Over the sound of the rushing stream, the Baudelaires heard a very dim sound coming from behind the hatch. The sound was a human voice, very deep and echoey as if it were coming from the bottom of a well. "Friend or foe?" it said.

The Baudelaires looked at one another. They knew, as I'm sure you know, that "friend or foe" is a traditional greeting directed at visitors who approach an important place, such as a royal palace or a fiercely guarded shoe store, and must identify themselves as either a friend or a foe of the people inside. But the siblings did not know if they were friends or foes for the simple reason that they had no idea who was talking.

"What should we say?" Violet asked, lowering her voice. "The eye might mean that it's Count Olaf's submarine, in which case we're foes."

"The eye might mean that it's V.F.D.'s submarine," Klaus said, "in which case we're friends."

"Obvio!" Sunny said, which meant "There's only one answer that will get us into the submarine," and she called down to the hatch, "Friend!"

There was a pause, and the echoey voice spoke again. "Password, please," it said.

The Baudelaires looked at one another again. A password, of course, is a certain word or phrase that one utters in order to receive information or enter a secret place, and the siblings of course had no idea what they should say in order to enter a submarine. For a moment none of the children said anything, merely tried to think, although they wished it were quieter so they could think without the distractions of the sounds of the rushing of water and the coughing of fish. They wished that instead of being stranded on a toboggan in the middle of the Stricken Stream, they were in some quiet room, such as the Baudelaire library, where they could sit in silence and read up on what the password might be. But as the three siblings thought of one library, one sibling remembered another: the ruined V.F.D. library, up in the Valley of Four Drafts where the headquarters had once stood. Violet thought of an iron archway, one of the few remnants of the library, and the motto that was etched into it. The eldest Baudelaire looked at her siblings and then leaned down to the hatch and repeated the mysterious words she had seen, and that she hoped would bring her and her siblings to safety.

"The world is quiet here," she said.

There was a pause, and with a loud, metallic *creak*, the hatch opened, and the siblings peered into a dark hole, which had a ladder running along the side so they could climb down. They shivered, and not just from the icy chill of the mountain winds and the rushing dark waters of the Stricken Stream. They shivered because they did not know where they were going, or who they might meet if they climbed down into the hole. Instead of entering, the Baudelaires wanted to call something else down the hatch— the same words that had been called up to them. "Friend or foe?" they wanted to say. "Friend or foe?" Would it be safer to enter the submarine, or safer to risk their lives outside, in the rushing waters of the Stricken Stream?

"Enter, Baudelaires," the voice said, and whether it belonged to friend or foe, the Baudelaires decided to climb inside.

CHAPTER
Two

"*Right* down here!" the echoey voice said, as the Baudelaire orphans began their journey down the ladder. "Aye! Mind the ladder! Close the hatch behind you! Don't rush! No—take your time! Don't fall! Mind your step! Aye! Don't trip! Don't make noise! Don't scare me! Don't look down! No—look where you're going! Don't bring any flammable liquids with you! Watch your feet! Aye! No—watch your back! No—watch your mouth! No—watch yourselves! Aye!"

"Aye?" Sunny whispered to her siblings.

" 'Aye,' " Klaus explained quietly, "is another word for 'yes.'"

"Aye!" the voice said again. "Keep your eyes open! Look out below! Look out above! Look out for spies! Look out for one another! Look out! Aye! Be very careful! Be very aware! Be very much! Take a break! No—keep going! Stay awake! Calm down! Cheer up! Keep climbing! Keep your shirt on! Aye!"

As desperate as their situation was, the Baudelaires almost found themselves giggling. The voice was shouting out so many instructions, and so few of them made sense, that it would have been impossible for the children to follow them, and the voice was quite cheerful and a bit scattered, as if whoever was talking did not really care if their instructions were followed and had probably forgotten them already. "Hold on to the railing!" the voice continued, as the Baudelaires spotted a light at the end of the passageway. "Aye! No—hold on to yourselves!

No—hold on to your hats! No—hold on to your hands! No—hold on! Wait a minute! Wait a second! Stop waiting! Stop war! Stop injustice! Stop bothering me! Aye!"

Sunny had been the first to enter the passageway, and so she was the first to reach the bottom and lower herself carefully into a small, dim room with a very low ceiling. Standing in the center of the room was an enormous man dressed in a shiny suit made of some sort of slippery-looking material with equally slippery-looking boots on his feet. On the front of the suit was a portrait of a man with a beard, although the man himself had no beard, merely a very long mustache curled up at both ends like a pair of parentheses. "One of you is a baby!" he cried, as Klaus and Violet lowered themselves next to their sister. "Aye! No—both of you are babies! No—there's three of you! No—none of you are babies! Well, one of you sort of is a baby! Welcome! Aye! Hello! Good afternoon! Howdy! Shake my hand! Aye!"

The Baudelaires hurriedly shook the man's hand, which was covered in a glove made of the same slippery material. "My name is Violet B—" Violet started to say.

"Baudelaire!" the man interrupted. "I know! I'm not stupid! Aye! And you're Klaus and Sunny! You're the Baudelaires! The three Baudelaire children! Aye! The ones *The Daily Punctilio* blames for every crime they can think of but you're really innocent but nevertheless in a big heap of trouble! Of course! Nice to meet you! In person! So to speak! Let's go! Follow me! Aye!"

The man whirled around and stomped out of the room, leaving the bewildered Baudelaires little else to do but follow him down a corridor. The corridor was covered in metal pipes that ran along the walls, floor, and ceiling, so that the Baudelaires sometimes had to duck, or step very high, in order to make their way. Occasionally drops of water would drip from one of the pipes and land on their heads, but they were already so damp from the Stricken Stream that they scarcely noticed. Besides, they were far too busy trying to follow what the man was saying to think of anything else.

"Let's see! I'll put you to work right away! Aye! No—first I'll give you a tour! No—I'll give you lunch! No—I'll introduce you to my crew! No—I'll let you rest! No—I'd better get you into uniforms! Aye! It's important that everyone aboard wear a waterproof uniform in case the submarine collapses and we find ourselves underwater! Of course, in that case we'll need diving helmets! Except Sunny because she can't wear one! I guess she'll drown! No—she can curl up inside a diving helmet! Aye! The helmets have a tiny door on the neck just for such a purpose! Aye! I've seen it done! I've seen so many things in my time!"

"Excuse me," Violet said, "but could you tell us who you are?"

The man whirled around to face the children and held his hands up over his head.

"*What?*" he roared. "You don't know who I am? I've never been so insulted in my life! No—I have. Many times, in fact. Aye! I remember when Count Olaf turned to me and said, in that horrible voice of his— No, never mind. I'll tell you. I'm Captain Widdershins. That's spelled W-I-D-D-E-R-S-H-I-N-S. Backward it's S-N-I-H-S-R—well, never mind. Nobody spells it backward! Except people who have no respect for the alphabet! And they're not here! Are they?"

"No," Klaus said. "We have a great deal of respect for the alphabet."

"I should say so!" the captain cried. "Klaus Baudelaire disrespect the alphabet? Why, it's unthinkable! Aye! It's illegal! It's impossible! It's not true! How dare you say so! No—you didn't say so! I apologize! One thousand pardons! Aye!"

"Is this your submarine, Captain Widdershins?" Violet asked.

"*What?*" the captain roared. "You don't know

whose submarine it is? A renowned inventor like yourself and you haven't the faintest sense of basic submarine history? Of course this is my submarine! It's been my submarine for years! Aye! Have you never heard of Captain Widdershins and the *Queequeg*? Have you never heard of the Submarine Q and Its Crew of Two? That's a little nickname I made up myself! With a little help! Aye! I would think Josephine would have told you about the *Queequeg*! After all, I patrolled Lake Lachrymose for years! Poor Josephine! There's not a day I don't think of her! Aye! Except some days when it slips my mind!"

"Nottooti?" Sunny asked.

"I was told it would take me some time to understand everything you said," the captain said, looking down at Sunny. "I'm not sure I'll find the time to learn another foreign language! Aye! Perhaps I could enroll in some night classes!"

"What my sister means," Violet said quickly,

"is that she's curious how you know so much about us."

"How does anyone know anything about anything?" the captain replied. "I read it, of course! Aye! I've read every Volunteer Factual Dispatch I've received! Although lately I haven't received any! Aye! That's why I'm glad you happened along! Aye! I thought I might faint when I peered through the periscope and saw your damp little faces staring back at me! Aye! I was sure it was you, but I didn't hesitate to ask you the password! Aye! I never hesitate! Aye! That's my personal philosophy!"

The captain stopped in the middle of the hallway, and pointed to a brass rectangle that was attached to a wall. It was a plaque, a word which here means "metal rectangle with words carved on it, usually to indicate that something important has happened on the spot where the rectangle is attached." This plaque had a large V.F.D. eye carved into the top, watching over the words THE CAPTAIN'S PERSONAL PHILOSOPHY carved in enormous letters, but the Baudelaires had to lean in close to see what was printed beneath it.

"'He who hesitates is lost'!" the captain cried, pointing at each word with a thick, gloved finger.

"'Or she,'" Violet added, pointing to a pair of words that someone had added in scratchy handwriting.

"My stepdaughter added that," Captain Widdershins said. "And she's right! 'Or she'! One day I was walking down this very hallway and I realized that anyone can be lost if they hesitate! A giant octopus could be chasing you, and if you decided to pause for a moment and tie your shoes, what would happen? All would be lost, that's what would happen! Aye! That's why it's my personal philosophy! I never hesitate! Never! Aye! Well, sometimes I do! But I try not to! Because He or she who hesitates is lost! Let's go!"

Without hesitating a moment longer at the

plaque, Captain Widdershins whirled around and led the children further down the corridor, which echoed with the odd sound of his waterproof boots each time he took a step. The children were a bit dizzy from the captain's chatter, and they were thinking about his personal philosophy and whether or not it ought to be their personal philosophies as well. Having a personal philosophy is like having a pet marmoset, because it may be very attractive when you acquire it, but there may be situations when it will not come in handy at all. "He or she who hesitates is lost" sounded like a reasonable philosophy at first glance, but the Baudelaires could think of situations in which hesitating might be the best thing to do. Violet was glad she'd hesitated when she and her siblings were living with Aunt Josephine, otherwise she might never have realized the importance of the peppermints she found in her pocket. Klaus was glad he'd hesitated at Heimlich Hospital, otherwise he might never have thought of a way to disguise Sunny and himself as medical professionals so they could rescue Violet from having unnecessary surgery. And Sunny was glad she'd hesitated outside Count Olaf's tent on Mount Fraught, otherwise she might never have overheard the name of the last safe place, which the Baudelaires still hoped to reach. But despite all these incidents in which hesitation had been very helpful, the children did not wish to adopt "He or she who does not hesitate is lost" as their personal philosophy, because a giant octopus might come along at any moment, particularly when the Baudelaires were on board a submarine, and the siblings would be very foolish to hesitate if the octopus were coming after them. Perhaps, the Baudelaires thought, the wisest personal philosophy concerning hesitation would be "Sometimes he or she should hesitate and sometimes he or she should not hesitate," but this seemed far too long and vague to be much use on a plaque.

"Maybe if I hadn't hesitated," the captain

continued, "the *Queequeg* would have been repaired by now! Aye! The Submarine Q and Its Crew of Two is not in the best of shape, I'm afraid! Aye! We've been attacked by villains and leeches, by sharks and realtors, by pirates and girlfriends, by torpedoes and angry salmon! Aye!" He stopped at a thick metal door, turned to the Baudelaires, and sighed. "Everything from the radar mechanisms to my alarm clock is malfunctioning! Aye! That's why I'm glad you're here, Violet Baudelaire! We're desperate for someone with mechanical smarts!"

"I'll see what I can do," Violet said.

"Well, take a look!" Captain Widdershins cried, and swung open the door. The Baudelaires followed him into an enormous, cavernous room that echoed when the captain spoke. There were pipes on the ceiling, pipes on the floor, and pipes sticking out of the walls at all angles. Between the pipes was a bewildering array of panels with knobs, gears, and tiny screens, as well as tiny signs saying things like,

DANGER!, WARNING!, and HE OR SHE WHO HESI-
TATES IS LOST! Here and there were a few green
lights, and at the far end was an enormous
wooden table piled with books, maps, and dirty
dishes, which stood beneath an enormous porthole, a word which here means "round window
through which the Baudelaires could see the
filthy waters of the Stricken Stream."

"This is the belly of the beast!" the captain
said. "Aye! It's the center of all operations
aboard the *Queequeg*! This is where we control
the submarine, eat our meals, research our missions, and play board games when we're tired of
working!" He strode over to one panel and
ducked his head beneath it. "Fiona!" he called.
"Come out of there!"

There was a faint rattling sound, and then
the children saw something race out from under
the panel and halfway across the floor. In the
dim green light it took a moment to see it was
a girl a bit older than Violet, who was lying
faceup on a small wheeled platform. She was

wearing a suit just like Captain Widdershins's, with the same portrait of the bearded man on the front, and had a flashlight in one hand and a pair of pliers in the other. Smiling, she handed the pliers to her stepfather, who helped her up from the platform as she put on a pair of eyeglasses with triangular frames.

"Baudelaires," the captain said, "this is Fiona, my stepdaughter. Fiona, this is Violet, Klaus, and Sunny Baudelaire."

"Charmed," she said, extending a gloved hand first to Violet, then to Klaus, and finally to Sunny, who gave Fiona a big toothy smile. "I'm sorry I wasn't upstairs to meet you. I've been trying to repair this telegram device, but electrical repairwork is not my specialty."

"Aye!" the captain said. "For quite some time we've stopped receiving telegrams, but Fiona can't seem to make heads or tails of the device! Violet, get to work!"

"You'll have to forgive the way my stepfather speaks," Fiona said, putting an arm around him. "It can take some getting used to."

"We don't have time to get used to any-thing!" Captain Widdershins cried. "This is no time to be passive! He who hesitates is lost!"

"Or she," Fiona corrected quietly. "Come on, Violet, I'll get you a uniform. If you're won-dering whose portrait is on the front, it's Her-man Melville."

"He's one of my favorite authors," Klaus said. "I really enjoy the way he dramatizes the plight of overlooked people, such as poor sailors or exploited youngsters, through his strange, often experimental philosophical prose."

"I should have known you liked him," Fiona replied. "When Josephine's house fell into the lake, my stepfather and I managed to save some of her library before it became too soaked. I read some of your decoding notes, Klaus. You're a very perceptive researcher."

"It's very kind of you to say so," Klaus said.

"Aye!" the captain cried. "A perceptive researcher is just what we need!" He stomped over to the table and lifted a pile of papers. "A certain taxi driver managed to smuggle these charts to me," he said, "but I can't make head or tail of them! They're confusing! They're confounding! They're conversational! No—that's not what I mean!"

"I think you mean *convoluted*," Klaus said, peering at the charts. "'Conversational' means 'having to do with conversations,' but 'convoluted' means 'complicated.' What kind of charts are they?"

"Tidal charts!" the captain cried. "We have to figure out the exact course of the predominant tides at the point where the Stricken Stream meets the sea! Klaus, I want you to find a uniform and then get to work immediately! Aye!"

"Aye!" Klaus said, trying to get into the spirit of the *Queequeg*.

"Aye!" the captain answered in a happy roar.

"I?" Sunny asked.

"Aye!" the captain said. "I haven't forgotten

you, Sunny! I'd never forget Sunny! Never in a million years! Not that I will live that long! Particularly because I don't exercise very much! But I don't like exercising, so it's worth it! Why, I remember when they wouldn't let me go mountain climbing because I hadn't trained properly, and—"

"Perhaps you should tell Sunny what you have in mind for her to do," Fiona said gently.

"Of course!" the captain cried. "Naturally! Our other crewman has been in charge of cooking, but all he does is make these terrible damp casseroles! I'm tired of them! I'm hoping your cooking skills might improve our meal situation!"

"Sous," Sunny said modestly, which meant something like, "I haven't been cooking for very long," and her siblings were quick to translate.

"Well, we're in a hurry!" the captain replied, walking over to a far door marked KITCHEN. "We can't wait for Sunny to become an expert chef before getting to work! He or she who hesitates is lost!" He opened the door and called inside. "Cookie! Get out here and meet the Baudelaires!"

The children heard some quiet, uneven footsteps, as if the cook had something wrong with one leg, and then a man limped through the door, wearing the same uniform as the captain and a wide smile on his face.

"Baudelaires!" he said. "I always believed I would see you again someday!"

The three siblings looked at the man and then at one another in stupefaction, a word which here means "amazement at seeing a man for the first time since their stay at Lucky Smells Lumbermill, when his kindness toward them had been one of the few positive aspects of that otherwise miserable chapter in their lives." "Phil!" Violet cried. "What on earth are you doing here?"

"He's the second of our crew of two!" the captain cried. "Aye! The original second in the crew of two was Fiona's mother, but she died in a manatee accident quite a few years ago."

"I'm not so sure it was an accident," Fiona said.

"Then we had Jacques!" the captain continued. "Aye, and then what's-his-name, Jacques's brother, and then a dreadful woman who turned out to be a spy, and finally we have Phil! Although I like to call him Cookie! I don't know why!"

"I was tired of working in the lumber industry," Phil said. "I was sure I could find a better job, and look at me now—cook on a dilapidated submarine. Life keeps on getting better and better."

"You always were an optimist," Klaus said.

"We don't need an optimist!" Captain Widdershins said. "We need a cook! Get to work, Baudelaires! All of you! Aye! We have no time to waste! He who hesitates is lost!"

"Or she," Fiona reminded her stepfather. "And do we really have to start right this minute? I'm sure the Baudelaires are exhausted from their journey. We could spend a nice quiet evening playing board games—"

"Board games?" the captain said in astonishment. "Amusements? Entertainments? We don't have time for such things! Aye! Today's Saturday, which means we only have five days left! Thursday is the V.F.D. gathering, and I don't want anyone at the Hotel Denouement to say that the *Queequeg* hasn't performed its mission!"

"Mission?" Sunny asked.

"Aye!" Captain Widdershins said. "We mustn't hesitate! We must act! We must hurry! We must move! We must search! We must investigate! We must hunt! We must pursue! We must stop occasionally for a brief snack! We must find that sugar bowl before Count Olaf does! Aye!"

CHAPTER

Three

The expression "Shiver me timbers!" comes from the society of pirates, who enjoy using interesting expressions almost as much as jumping aboard other people's ships and stealing their valuables. It is an expression of extreme amazement, used in circumstances when one feels as if one's very bones, or timbers, are shivering. I have not used the expression since one rainy night when it was necessary to pose as a pirate experiencing amazement, but when Captain Widdershins told the Baudelaire orphans where the *Queequeg* was going and what it was searching for, there was a perfect opportunity to utter these words.

"Shiver me timbers!" Sunny cried.

"Your timbers!" the captain cried back. "Are the Baudelaires practicing piracy? Aye! My heavens! If your parents knew that you were stealing the treasures of others—"

"We're not pirates, Captain Widdershins," Violet said hastily. "Sunny is just using an expression she learned from an old movie. She just means that we're surprised."

"Surprised?" The captain paced up and down in front of them, his waterproof suit crinkling with every step. "Do you think the *Queequeg* made its difficult way up the Stricken Stream just for my own personal amusement? Aye? Do you think I would risk such terrible danger simply because I had no other plans for the afternoon? Aye? Do you think it was a crazy coincidence that you ran into our periscope? Aye? Do you think this uniform makes me look fat? Aye? Do you think members of V.F.D.

would just sit and twiddle their thumbs while Count Olaf's treachery covers the land like crust covers the filling of a pie? Aye?"

"You were looking for us?" Klaus asked in amazement. He was tempted to cry "Shiver me timbers!" like his sister, but he did not want to alarm Captain Widdershins any further.

"For you!" the captain cried. "Aye! For the sugar bowl! Aye! For justice! Aye! And liberty! Aye! For an opportunity to make the world quiet! Aye! And safe! Aye! And we may only have until Thursday! Aye! We're in terrible danger! Aye! So get to work!"

"Bamboozle!" Sunny cried.

"My sister is confused," Violet said, "and so are we, Captain Widdershins. If we could just stop for a moment, and hear your story from the beginning—"

"Stop for a moment?" the captain repeated in astonishment. "I've just explained our desperate circumstances, and you're asking me to hesitate? My dear girl, remember my personal philosophy! Aye! 'He or she who hesitates is lost'! Now let's get moving!"

The children looked at one another in frustration. They did not want to get moving. It felt to the Baudelaire orphans that they had been moving almost constantly since that terrible day at the beach when their lives had been turned upside down. They had moved into Count Olaf's home, and then into the homes of various guardians. They had moved away from a village intent on burning them at the stake, and they had moved into a hospital that had burst into flames around them. They had moved to the hinterlands in the trunk of Count Olaf's car, and they had moved away from the hinterlands in disguise. They had moved up the Mortmain Mountains hoping to find one of their parents, and they had moved down the Mortmain Mountains thinking they would never see their parents again, and now, in a tiny submarine in the Stricken Stream, they wanted to stop moving, just for a little while, and receive some answers to questions they had been asking themselves since all this moving began.

"Stepfather," Fiona said gently, "why don't you start up the *Queequeg*'s engines, and I'll show the Baudelaires where our spare uniforms are?"

"I'm the captain!" the captain announced. "Aye! I'll give the orders around here!" Then he shrugged, and squinted up toward the ceiling. The Baudelaires noticed for the first time a ladder of rope running up the side of wall. It led up to a small shelf, where the children could see a large wheel, probably for steering, and a few rusty levers and switches that were Byzantine in their design, a phrase which here means "so complicated that perhaps even Violet Baudelaire would have trouble working them." "I order myself to go up the ladder," the captain continued a bit sheepishly, "and start the engines of the *Queequeg*." With one last "Aye!" the captain began hoisting himself toward the ceiling, and the Baudelaires were left alone with Fiona and Phil.

"You must be overwhelmed, Baudelaires," Phil said. "I remember my first day aboard the *Queequeg*—it made Lucky Smells Lumbermill seem calm and quiet!"

"Phil, why don't you get the Baudelaires some soda, while I find them some uniforms?" Fiona said.

"Soda?" Phil said, with a nervous glance at the captain, who was already halfway up the ladder. "We're supposed to save the soda for a special occasion."

"It *is* a special occasion," Fiona said. "We're welcoming three more volunteers on board. What kind of soda do you prefer, Baudelaires?"

"Anything but parsley," Violet said, referring to a beverage enjoyed by Esmé Squalor.

"I'll bring you some lemon-lime," Phil said. "Sailors should always make sure there's plenty of citrus in their system. I'm so glad to see you, children. You know, I wouldn't be here if it weren't for you. I was so horrified after what happened in Paltryville that I couldn't stay at

Lucky Smells, and since then my life has been one big adventure!"

"I'm sorry that your leg never healed," Klaus said, referring to Phil's limp. "I didn't realize the accident with the stamping machine was so serious."

"That's not why I'm limping," Phil said. "I was bitten by a shark last week. It was very painful, but I'm quite lucky. Most people never get an opportunity to get so close to such a deadly animal!"

The Baudelaires watched him as he limped back through the kitchen door, whistling a bouncy tune. "Was Phil always optimistic when you knew him?" Fiona asked.

"Always," Violet said, and her siblings nodded in agreement. "We've never known anyone who could remain so cheerful, no matter what terrible things occurred."

"To tell you the truth, I sometimes find it a bit tiresome," Fiona said, adjusting her triangular glasses. "Shall we find you some uniforms?"

The Baudelaires nodded, and followed Fiona out of the Main Hall and back into the narrow corridor. "I know you have a lot of questions," she said, "so I'll try to tell you everything I know. My stepfather believes that he or she who hesitates is lost, but I have a more cautious personal philosophy."

"We'd be very grateful if you might tell us a few things," Klaus said. "First, how do you know who we are? Why were you looking for us? How did you know how to find us?"

"That's a lot of firsts," Fiona said with a smile. "I think you Baudelaires are forgetting that your exploits haven't exactly been a secret. Nearly every day there's been a story about you in one of the most popular newspapers."

"*The Daily Punctilio?*" Violet asked. "I hope you haven't been believing the dreadful lies they've been printing about us."

"Of course not," Fiona said. "But even the most ridiculous of stories can contain a grain of truth. *The Daily Punctilio* said that you'd murdered a man in the Village of Fowl Devotees, and then set fires at Heimlich Hospital and Caligari Carnival. We knew, of course, that you hadn't committed these crimes, but we could tell that you had been there. My stepfather and I figured that you'd found the secret stain on Madame Lulu's map, and were headed for the V.F.D. headquarters."

Klaus gasped. "You know about Madame Lulu," he said, "and the coded stain?"

"My stepfather taught that code to Madame Lulu," Fiona explained, "a long time ago, when they were both young. Well, we heard about the destruction of the headquarters, so we assumed that you'd be heading back down the mountain. So I set a course for the *Queequeg* to journey up the Stricken Stream."

"You traveled all the way up here," Klaus said, "just to find us?"

Fiona looked down. "Well, no," she said. "You weren't the only thing at V.F.D. headquarters. One of our Volunteer Factual Dispatches told us that the sugar bowl was there as well."

"Dephinpat?" Sunny asked.

"What are Volunteer Factual Dispatches, exactly?" Violet translated.

"They're a way of sharing information," Fiona said. "It's difficult for volunteers to meet up with one another, so when they unlock a mystery they can write it in a telegram. That way, important information gets circulated, and before long our commonplace books will be full of information we can use to defeat our enemies. A commonplace book is a—"

"We know what a commonplace book is," Klaus said, and removed his dark blue notebook from his pocket. "I've been keeping one myself."

Fiona smiled, and drummed her gloved fingers on the cover of Klaus's book. "I should have known," she said. "If your sisters want to start books themselves, we should have a few spares. Everything's in our supply room."

"So are we going up to the ruins of the headquarters," Violet asked, "to get the sugar bowl?

We didn't see it there."

"We think someone threw it out the window," Fiona answered, "when the fire began. If they threw the sugar bowl from the kitchen, it would have landed in the Stricken Stream and been carried by the water cycle all the way down the mountains. We were seeing if it could be found at the bottom of the stream when we happened upon you three."

"The stream probably carried it much further than this," Klaus said thoughtfully.

"I think so too," Fiona agreed. "I'm hoping that you can discover its location by studying my stepfather's tidal charts. I can't make head or tail of them."

"I'll show you how to read them," Klaus said. "It's not difficult."

"That's what frightens me," Fiona said. "If those charts aren't difficult to read, then Count Olaf might have a chance of finding the sugar bowl before we do. My stepfather says that if the sugar bowl falls into his hands, then all of the efforts of all of the volunteers will be for naught."

The Baudelaires nodded, and the four children made their way down the corridor in silence. The phrase "for naught" is simply a fancy way of saying "for nothing," and it doesn't matter which phrase you use, for they are both equally difficult to admit. Later this afternoon, for instance, I will enter a large room full of sand, and if I do not find the test tube I am looking for, it will be difficult to admit that I have sifted through all that sand for nothing. If you insist on finishing this book, you will find it difficult to admit, between bouts of weeping, that you have read this story for naught, and that it would have been better to page through tedious descriptions of the water cycle. And the Baudelaires did not want to find themselves admitting that all of their troubles had been for naught, that all their adventures meant nothing, and that their entire lives were naught and nothing, if Count Olaf managed to find this crucial sugar bowl before they did. The three siblings followed Fiona down the dim corridor and hoped that their time aboard the *Queequeg* would not be another terrifying journey ending in more disappointment, disillusionment, and despair.

For the moment, however, their journey ended at a small door where Fiona stopped and turned to face the Baudelaires. "This is our supply room," she said. "Inside you'll find uniforms for the three of you, although even our smallest size might be too big for Sunny."

"Pinstripe," Sunny said. She meant something like, "Don't worry—I'm used to ill-fitting clothing," and her siblings were quick to translate.

"You'll need diving helmets, too," Fiona said. "This is an old submarine, and it could spring a leak. If the leak is serious, the pressure of the water could cause the walls of the *Queequeg* to collapse, filling all these rooms and corridors with water. The oxygen systems contained in the diving helmets enable you to breathe underwater—for a short time, anyway."

"Your stepfather said that the helmets would be too big for Sunny, and that she'd have to curl up inside one," Violet said. "Is that safe?"

"Safe but uncomfortable," Fiona said, "like everything else on the *Queequeg*. This submarine used to be in wonderful shape, but without anyone who knows about mechanics, it's not quite up to its former glory. Many of the rooms have flooded, so I'm sorry to say that we'll be sleeping in very tight quarters. I hope you like bunk beds."

"We've slept on worse," Klaus said.

"So I hear," Fiona replied. "I read a description of the Orphans Shack at Prufrock Preparatory School. That sounded terrible."

"So you knew about us, even then?" Violet asked. "Why didn't you find us sooner?"

Fiona sighed. "We knew about you," she said. "Every day I would read terrible stories in the newspaper, but my stepfather said we couldn't do anything about all the treachery those stories contained."

"Why not?" Klaus asked.

"He said your troubles were too enormous," she replied.

"I don't understand," Violet said.

"I don't really understand, either," Fiona admitted. "My stepfather said that the amount of treachery in this world is enormous, and that the best we could do was one small noble thing. That's why we're looking for the sugar bowl. You'd think that accomplishing such a small task would be easy, but we've been looking for ages and still haven't found it."

"But what's so important about the sugar bowl?" Klaus asked.

Fiona sighed again, and blinked several times behind her triangular glasses. She looked so sad that the middle Baudelaire almost wished he hadn't asked. "I don't know," she said. "He won't tell me."

"Whyno?" Sunny asked.

"He said it was better I didn't know," Fiona said. "I guess that's enormous, too—an enormous secret. He said people had been destroyed for knowing such enormous secrets, and that he didn't want me in that sort of danger."

"But you're already in danger," Klaus said. "We're all in danger. We're on board an unstable submarine, trying to find a tiny, important object before a nefarious villain gets his hands on it."

Fiona turned the handle of the door, which opened with a long, loud *creak* that made the Baudelaires shiver. The room was very small and very dim, lit only by one small green light, and for a moment, it looked like the room was full of people staring silently at the children in the corridor. But then the siblings saw it was just a row of uniforms, hanging limply from hooks along the wall. "I guess there are worse dangers," Fiona said quietly. "I guess there are dangers we simply can't imagine."

The Baudelaires looked at their companion

and then at the eerie row of empty uniforms.
On a shelf above the waterproof suits was a
row of large diving helmets, round spheres of
metal with small circular windows in the
middle so the children would be able to see out
when they put them on. In the dim green light,
the helmets looked a bit like eyes, glaring
at the Baudelaires from the supply room just
as the eye on Count Olaf's ankle had glared at
them so many times before. Although they still
weren't pirates, the siblings were tempted to
say "shiver me timbers" once again as they
stepped inside the small, cramped room, and
felt themselves shiver down to their bones.
They did not like to think about the *Queequeg*
springing a leak or collapsing, or to imagine
themselves frantically attaching the diving helmets to their heads—or, in Sunny's case, frantically stuffing herself inside. They did not like
to think about where Count Olaf might be, or
imagine what would happen if he found the
sugar bowl before they did. But most of all, the

Baudelaire orphans did not like to think about the dangers Fiona had mentioned—dangers worse than the ones they faced, or dangers they simply couldn't imagine.

CHAPTER Four

The expression "fits like a glove" is an odd one, because there are many different types of gloves and only a few of them are going to fit the situation you are in. If you need to keep your hands warm in a cold environment, then you'll need a fitted pair of insulated gloves, and a glove made to fit in the bureau of a dollhouse will be of no help whatsoever. If you need to sneak into a restaurant in the middle of the night and steal a pair of chopsticks without being discovered, then you'll need a sheer pair of gloves that leave

no marks, and a glove decorated with loud bells simply will not do. And if you need to pass unnoticed in a shrubbery-covered landscape, then you'll need a very, very large glove made of green and leafy fabric, and an elegant pair of silk gloves will be entirely useless.

Nevertheless, the expression "fits like a glove" simply means that something is very suitable, the way a custard is suitable for dessert, or a pair of chopsticks is a suitable tool to remove papers from an open briefcase, and when the Baudelaire orphans put on the uniforms of the *Queequeg* they found that they fitted the children like a glove, despite the fact that they did not actually fit that well. Violet was so pleased that the uniforms had several loops around the waist, just perfect for holding tools, that she didn't care that her sleeves bagged at the elbows. Klaus was happy that there was a waterproof pocket for his commonplace book, and didn't care that his boots were a bit too tight. And Sunny was reassured that the shiny material was sturdy enough to resist cooking spills as well as water, and didn't mind rolling up the legs of the suit almost all the way so she could walk. But it was more than the individual features of the uniforms that felt fitting—it was the place and the people they represented. For a long time the Baudelaires had felt as if their lives were a damaged Frisbee, tossed from person to person and from place to place without ever really being appreciated or fitting in. But as they zipped up their uniforms and smoothed out the portraits of Herman Melville, the children felt as if the Frisbee of their lives just might be repaired. In wearing the uniform of the *Queequeg*, the siblings felt a part of something—not a family, exactly, but a gathering of people who had all volunteered for the same mission. To think that their skills in inventing, research, and cooking would be appreciated was something they had not thought in a long time, and as they stood in the supply room and regarded one another, this feeling fit them like a glove.

"Shall we go back to the Main Hall?" Violet asked. "I'm ready to take a look at the telegram device."

"Let me just loosen the buckles on these boots," Klaus said, "and I'll be ready to tackle those tidal charts."

"Cuisi—" Sunny said. By "Cuisi," she meant something like, "I'm looking forward to examining the kitch—" but a loud scraping sound from overhead stopped the youngest Baudelaire from finishing her sentence. The entire submarine seemed to shake, and a few drops of water fell from the ceiling onto the Baudelaires' heads.

"What was that?" Violet asked, picking up a diving helmet. "Do you think the *Queequeg* has sprung a leak?"

"I don't know," Klaus said, picking up one helmet for himself and another for Sunny. "Let's go find out."

The three Baudelaires hurried back down the corridor to the Main Hall as the horrid scraping sound continued. If you have ever heard the sound of fingernails against a chalkboard, then you know how unnerving a scraping sound can be, and to the children it sounded as if the largest fingernails in the world had mistaken the submarine for a piece of educational equipment.

"Captain Widdershins!" Violet cried over the scraping sound as the Baudelaires entered the hall. The captain was still at the top of the ladder, grasping the steering wheel in his gloved hand. "What's going on?"

"This darned steering mechanism is a disgrace!" the captain cried in disgust. "Aye! The *Queequeg* just bumped against a rock formation on the side of the stream. If I hadn't managed to get the sub back in control, the Submarine Q and Its Crew of Two would be sleeping with the fishes! Aye!"

"Perhaps I should examine the steering mechanism first," Violet said, "and fix the telegram device later."

"Don't be ridiculous!" the captain said. "If we can't receive any Volunteer Factual Dispatches, we might as well be wandering around with our eyes closed! We must find the sugar bowl before Count Olaf! Aye! Our personal safety isn't nearly as important! Now hurry up! Aye! Get a move on! Aye! Get cracking! Aye! Get a glass of water if you're thirsty! Aye! He or she who hesitates is lost!"

Violet didn't bother to point out that finding the sugar bowl would be impossible if the submarine was destroyed, and she knew better than to argue with the captain's personal philosophy. "It's worth a try," she said, and walked over to the small wheeled platform. "Do you mind if I use this?" she asked Fiona. "It'll help me get a good look at the device's machinery."

"Be my guest," Fiona said. "Klaus, let's get to work on the tidal charts. We can study them at the table, and keep an eye out for glimpses of the sugar bowl through the porthole. I don't think we'll see it, but it's worth taking a look."

"Fiona," Violet said hesitantly, "could you

also take a look for our friend, Quigley Quagmire? He was carried away by the stream's other tributary, and we haven't seen him since."

"Quigley Quagmire?" Fiona asked. "The cartographer?"

"He's a friend of ours," Klaus said. "Do you know him?"

"Only by reputation," Fiona said, using a phrase which here means "I don't know him personally but I've heard of the work he does." "The volunteers lost track of him a long time ago, along with Hector and the other Quagmire triplets."

"The Quagmires haven't been as lucky as we have," Violet said, tying her hair up in a ribbon to help her focus on repairing the telegram device. "I'm hoping you'll spot him with the periscope."

"It's worth a try," Fiona said, as Phil walked through the kitchen doors, wearing an apron over his uniform.

"Sunny?" he asked. "I heard you were going to help me in the kitchen. We're a bit low on supplies, I'm afraid. Using the *Queequeg* nets I managed to catch a few cod, and we have half a sack of potatoes, but not much else. Do you have any ideas about what to make for dinner?"

"Chowda?" Sunny asked.

"It's worth a try," Phil said, and for the next few hours, all three Baudelaires tried to see if their tasks were worth a try. Violet wheeled herself underneath several pipes to get a good look at the telegram device, and frowned as she twisted wires and tightened a few screws with a screwdriver she found lying around. Klaus sat at the table and looked over the tidal charts, using a pencil to trace possible paths the sugar bowl might have taken as the water cycle sent it tumbling down the Stricken Stream. And Sunny worked with Phil, standing on a large soup pot so she could reach the counter of the small, grimy kitchen, boiling potatoes and picking tiny bones out of the cod. And as the afternoon turned to evening, and the waters of the Stricken Stream grew even darker in the porthole, the Main Hall of the *Queequeg* was quiet as all the volunteers worked on the tasks at hand. But even when Captain Widdershins climbed down from the ladder, retrieved a small bell from a pocket of his uniform, and filled the room with the echoes of its loud, metallic ring, the Baudelaires could not be certain if all their efforts had been worth a try at all.

"Attention!" the captain said. "Aye! I want the entire crew of the *Queequeg* to report on their progress! Gather 'round the table and tell me what's going on!"

Violet wheeled herself out from under the telegram device, and joined her brother and Fiona at the table, while Sunny and Phil emerged from the kitchen.

"I'll report first!" the captain said. "Aye! Because I'm the captain! Not because I'm showing off! Aye! I try not to show off very much! Aye! Because it's rude! Aye! I've managed to steer us further down the Stricken Stream without bumping into anything else! Aye! Which is much harder than it sounds! Aye! We've reached the sea! Aye! Now it should be easier not to run into anything! Aye! Violet, what about you?"

"Well, I thoroughly examined the telegram device," Violet said. "I made a few minor repairs, but I found nothing that would interfere with receiving a telegram."

"You're saying that the device isn't broken, aye?" the captain demanded.

"Aye," Violet said, growing more comfortable with the captain's speech. "I think there must be a problem at the other end."

"Procto?" Sunny asked, which meant "The other end?"

"A telegram requires two devices," Violet said. "One to send the message and the other to receive it. I think you haven't been receiving Volunteer Factual Dispatches because whoever sends the messages is having a problem with their machine."

"But all sorts of volunteers send us messages," Fiona said.

"Aye!" the captain said. "We've received dispatches from more than twenty-five agents!"

"Then many machines must be damaged," Violet replied.

"Sabotage," Klaus said.

"It does sound like the damage has been done on purpose," Violet agreed. "Remember when we sent a telegram to Mr. Poe, from the Last Chance General Store?"

"Silencio," Sunny said, which meant "We never heard a reply."

"They're closing in," the captain said darkly. "Our enemies are preventing us from communicating."

"I don't see how Count Olaf would have time to destroy all those machines," Klaus said.

"Many telegrams travel through telephone

lines," Fiona said. "It wouldn't be difficult."

"Besides, Olaf isn't the only enemy," Violet said, thinking of two other villains the Baudelaires had encountered on Mount Fraught.

"Aye!" the captain said. "That's for certain. There is evil out there you cannot even imagine. Klaus, have you made any progress on the tidal charts?"

Klaus spread out a chart on the table so everyone could see. The chart was really more of a map, showing the Stricken Stream winding through the mountains before reaching the sea, with tiny arrows and notations describing the way the water was moving. The arrows and notes were in several different colors of ink, as if the chart had been passed from researcher to researcher, each adding notes as he or she discovered more information about the area. "It's more complicated than I thought," the middle Baudelaire said, "and much more dull. These charts note every single detail concerning the water cycle."

"*Dull?*" the captain roared. "Aye? We're in the middle of a desperate mission and all you can think of is your own entertainment? Aye? Do you want us to *hesitate*? Stop our activities and put on a puppet show just so you won't find this submarine *dull?*"

"You misunderstood me," Klaus said quickly. "All I meant was that it's easier to research something that's interesting."

"You sound like Fiona," the captain said. "When I want her to research the life of Herman Melville, she works slowly, but she's quick as a whip when the subject is mushrooms."

"Mushrooms?" Klaus asked. "Are you a mycologist?"

Fiona smiled, and her eyes grew wide behind her triangular glasses. "I never thought I'd meet someone who knew that word," she said. "Besides me. Yes, I'm a mycologist. I've been interested in fungi all my life. If we have time, I'll show you my mycological library."

"*Time?*" Captain Widdershins repeated. "We

don't have time for fungus books! Aye! We don't have time for you two to do all that flirting, either!"

"We're not *flirting*!" Fiona said. "We're having a conversation."

"It looked like flirting to me," the captain said. "Aye!"

"Why don't you tell us about your research," Violet said to Klaus, knowing that her brother would rather talk about the tidal charts than his personal life. Klaus gave her a grateful smile and pointed to a point on the chart.

"If my calculations are correct," he said, "the sugar bowl would have been carried down the same tributary we went down in the toboggan. The prevailing currents of the stream lead all the way down here, where the sea begins."

"So it was carried out to sea," Violet said.

"I think so," Klaus said. "And we can see here that the tides would move it away from Sontag Shore in a northeasterly direction."

"Sink?" Sunny asked, which meant something like, "Wouldn't the sugar bowl just drift to the ocean floor?"

"It's too small," Klaus said. "Oceans are in constant motion, and an object that falls into the sea could end up miles away. It appears that the tides and currents in this part of the ocean would take the sugar bowl past the Gulag Archipelago here, and then head down toward the Mediocre Barrier Reef before turning at this point here, which is marked 'A.A.' Do you know what that is, Captain? It looks like some sort of floating structure."

The captain sighed, and raised one finger to fiddle with the curl of his mustache. "Aye," he said sadly. "Anwhistle Aquatics. It's a marine research center and a rhetorical advice service— or it *was*. It burned down."

"Anwhistle?" Violet asked. "That was Aunt Josephine's last name."

"Aye," the captain said. "Anwhistle Aquatics was founded by Gregor Anwhistle, the famous ichnologist and Josephine's brother-in-law. But all that's ancient history. Where did the sugar bowl go next?"

The Baudelaires would have preferred to learn more, but knew better than to argue with the captain, and Klaus pointed to a small oval on the chart to continue his report. "This is the part that confuses me," he said. "You see this oval, right next to Anwhistle Aquatics? It's marked 'G.G.,' but there's no other explanation."

"G.G.?" Captain Widdershins said, and stroked his mustache thoughtfully. "I've never seen an oval like that on a chart like this."

"There's something else confusing about it," Klaus said, peering at the oval. There are two different arrows inside it, and each one points in a different direction."

"It looks like the tide is going two ways at once," Fiona said.

Violet frowned. "That doesn't make any sense," she said.

"I'm confused, too," Klaus said. "According to my calculations, the sugar bowl was probably carried right to this place on the map. But where it went from there I can't imagine."

"I guess we should set a course for G.G., whatever it might be," Violet said, "and see what we can find when we get there."

"I'm the captain!" the captain cried. "I'll give the orders around here! Aye! And I order that we set a course for that oval, and see what we can find when we get there! But first I'm hungry! And thirsty! Aye! And my arm itches! I can scratch my own arm, but Cookie and Sunny, you are responsible for food and drink! Aye!"

"Sunny helped me make a chowder that should be ready in a few minutes," Phil said. "Her teeth were very handy in dicing the boiled potatoes."

"Flosh," Sunny said, which meant "Don't worry—I cleaned my teeth before using them as kitchen implements."

"Chowder? Aye! Chowder sounds delicious!" the captain cried. "And what about dessert? Aye? Dessert is the most important meal of the day!

Aye! In my opinion! Even though it's not really a meal! Aye!"

"Tonight, the only dessert we have is gum," Phil said. "I still have some left from my days at the lumbermill."

"I think I'll pass on dessert," Klaus said, who'd had such a terrible time at Lucky Smells Lumbermill that he no longer had a taste for gum.

"Yomhuledet," Sunny said. She meant "Don't worry—Phil and I have arranged a surprise dessert for tomorrow night," but of course only her siblings could understand the youngest Baudelaire's unusual way of talking. Nevertheless, as soon as Sunny spoke, Captain Widdershins stood up from the table and began crying out in astonishment.

"Aye!" he cried. "Dear God! Holy Buddha! Charles Darwin! Duke Ellington! Aye! Fiona—turn off the engines! Aye! Cookie—turn off the stove! Aye! Violet—make sure the telegram device is off! Aye! Klaus! Gather your materials together so nothing rolls around! Aye! Calm down! Work quickly! Don't panic! Help! Aye!"

"What's going on?" Phil asked.

"What is it, stepfather?" Fiona asked.

For once, the captain was silent, and merely pointed at a screen on the submarine wall. The screen looked like a piece of graph paper, lit up in green light, with a glowing letter Q in the center.

"That looks like a sonar detector," Violet said.

"It *is* a sonar detector," Fiona said. "We can tell if any other undersea craft are approaching us by detecting the sounds they make. The Q represents the *Queequeg* and—"

The mycologist gasped, and the Baudelaires looked at where she was pointing. At the very top of the panel was another glowing symbol, which was moving down the screen at a fast clip, a phrase which here means "straight toward the *Queequeg*." Fiona did not say what this green symbol stood for, and the children could not bear to ask. It was an eye, staring at the frightened volunteers and wiggling its long, skinny eyelashes, which protruded from every side.

"Olaf!" Sunny said in a whisper.

"There's no way of knowing for sure," Fiona said, "but we'd better follow my stepfather's orders. If it's another submarine, then it has a sonar detector too. If the *Queequeg* is absolutely silent, they'll have no idea we're here."

"Aye!" the captain said. "Hurry! He who hesitates is lost!"

Nobody bothered to add "Or she" to the captain's personal philosophy, but instead hurried to silence the submarine. Fiona climbed up the rope ladder and turned off the whirring engine. Violet wheeled back into the machinery of the telegram device and turned it off. Phil and Sunny ran into the kitchen to turn off the stove, so even the bubbling of their homemade chowder would not give the *Queequeg* away. And Klaus and the captain gathered up the materials on the table so that nothing would make even the slightest rattle. Within moments the submarine was silent as the grave, and all the volunteers stood mutely at the table, looking out the porthole into the gloomy water of the sea. As the eye on the sonar screen drew closer to the Q, they could see something emerge from the darkened waters—a strange shape that became clearer as it got closer and closer to the *Queequeg*. It was, indeed, another submarine, the likes of which the Baudelaires had never seen before, even in the strangest of books. It was much, much bigger than the *Queequeg*, and as it approached, the children had to cover their mouths so their gasps could not be heard.

The second submarine was in the shape of a giant octopus, with an enormous metal dome for a head and two wide portholes for eyes. A real octopus, of course, has eight legs, but this submarine had many more. What had appeared to be eyelashes on the sonar screen were really small metal tubes, protruding from the body of the octopus and circling in the water, making thousands of bubbles that hurried toward the surface as if they were frightened of the underwater craft. The octopus drew closer, and all six passengers on the *Queequeg* stood as still as statues, hoping the submarine had not discovered them. The strange craft was so close the Baudelaires could see a shadowy figure inside one of the octopus's eyes—a tall, lean figure, and although the children could not see any further details, they were positive the figure had one eyebrow instead of two, filthy fingernails instead of good grooming habits, and a tattoo of an eye on its left ankle.

"Count Olaf," Sunny whispered, before she could stop herself. The figure in the porthole twitched, as if Sunny's tiny noise had caused the *Queequeg* to be detected. Spouting more bubbles, the octopus drew closer still, and any moment it seemed that one of the legs of the octopus would be heard scraping against the outside of the *Queequeg*. The three children looked down at their helmets, which they had left on the floor, and wondered if they should put them on, so they might survive if the submarine collapsed. Fiona grabbed her stepfather's arm, but Captain Widdershins shook his head silently, and pointed at the sonar screen again. The eye and the Q were almost on top of one another on the screen, but that was not what the captain was pointing at.

There was a third shape of glowing green light, this one the biggest of all, a huge curved tube with a small circle at the end of it, slithering toward the center of the screen like a snake. But this third underwater craft didn't look like a snake. As it approached the eye and the Q, the small circle leading the enormous curved tube toward the *Queequeg* and its frightened volunteer crew, the shape looked more like a question mark. The Baudelaires stared at this new, third shape approaching them in eerie silence, and felt as if they were about to be consumed by the very questions they were trying to answer.

Captain Widdershins pointed at the porthole

again, and the children watched the octopus stop, as if it too had detected this strange third shape. Then the legs of the octopus began whirring even more furiously, and the strange submarine began to recede from view, a phrase which here means "disappear from the porthole as it hurried away from the *Queequeg*." The Baudelaires looked at the sonar screen, and watched the question mark follow the glowing green eye in silence until both shapes disappeared from the sonar detector and the *Queequeg* was alone. The six passengers waited a moment and then sighed with relief.

"It's gone," Violet said. "Count Olaf didn't find us."

"I knew we'd be safe," Phil said, optimistic as usual. "Olaf is probably in a good mood anyway."

The Baudelaires did not bother to say that their enemy was only in a good mood when one of his treacherous plans was succeeding, or when the enormous fortune, left behind by the Baudelaire parents, appeared to be falling into his grubby hands.

"What was that, Stepfather?" Fiona said. "Why did he leave?"

"What was that third shape?" Violet asked.

The captain shook his head again. "Something very bad," he said. "Even worse than Olaf, probably. I told you Baudelaires that there is evil you cannot even imagine."

"We don't have to imagine it," Klaus said. "We saw it there on the screen."

"That screen is nothing," the captain said. "It's just a piece of equipment, aye? There was a philosopher who said that all of life is just shadows. He said that people were just sitting in a cave, watching shadows on the cave wall. Aye—shadows of something much bigger and grander than themselves. Well, that sonar detector is like our cave wall, showing us the shape of things much more powerful and terrifying."

"I don't understand," Fiona said.

"I don't want you to understand," the captain said, putting his arm around her. "That's why I haven't told you why the sugar bowl is so very crucial. There are secrets in this world too terrible for young people to know, even as those secrets get closer and closer. Aye! In any case, I'm hungry. Aye! Shall we eat?"

The captain rang his bell again, and the Baudelaires felt as if they had awoken from a deep sleep. "I'll serve the chowder," Phil said. "Come on, Sunny, why don't you help me?"

"I'll turn the engines back on," Fiona said, and began climbing the rope ladder. "Violet, there's a drawer in the table full of silverware. Perhaps you and your brother could set the table."

"Of course," Violet said, but then frowned as she turned to her brother. The middle Baudelaire was staring at the tidal chart with a look of utter concentration. His eyes were so bright behind his glasses that they looked a bit like the glowing symbols on the sonar detector. "Klaus?" she said.

Klaus didn't answer his sister, but turned his gaze from the chart to Captain Widdershins. "I may not know why the sugar bowl's important," he said, "but I've just figured out where it is."

CHAPTER Five

When you are invited to dine, particularly with
people you do not know very well, it always
helps to have a conversational opener, a phrase
which here means "an interesting sentence to
say out loud in order to get people talking."
Although lately it has become more and more
difficult to attend dinner parties without the
evening ending in gunfire

or tapioca, I keep a list of good and bad conversational openers in my commonplace book in order to avoid awkward pauses at the dinner table. "Who would like to see an assortment of photographs taken while I was on vacation?" for instance, is a very poor conversational opener, because it is likely to make your fellow diners shudder instead of talk, whereas good conversational openers are sentences such as "What would drive a man to commit arson?," "Why do so many stories of true love end in tragedy and despair?," and "Madame diLustro, I believe I've discovered your true identity!," all of which are likely to provoke discussions, arguments, and accusations, thus making the dinner party much more entertaining. When Klaus Baudelaire announced that he'd discovered the location of the sugar bowl, it was one of the best conversational openers in the history of dinner gatherings, because everyone aboard the *Queequeg* began talking at once, and dinner had not even been served.

"Aye?" Captain Widdershins shouted. "You've figured out where the tide took it? Aye? But you just said you didn't know! Aye! You said you were confused by the tidal charts, and that oval marked 'G.G.'! Aye! And yet you've figured it out! Aye! You're a genius! Aye! You're a smarty-pants! Aye! You're a bookworm! Aye! You're brilliant! Aye! You're sensational! Aye! If you find me the sugar bowl, I'll allow you to marry Fiona!"

"Stepfather!" Fiona cried, blushing behind her triangular glasses.

"Don't worry," the captain replied, "we'll find a husband for Violet, too! Aye! Perhaps we'll find your long-lost brother, Fiona! He's much older, of course, and he's been missing for years, but if Klaus can locate the sugar bowl he could probably find him! Aye! He's a charming man, so you'd probably fall in love with him, Violet, and then we could have a double wedding! Aye! Right here in the Main Hall of the *Queequeg*! Aye! I would be happy to officiate!

Aye! I have a bow tie I've been saving for a special occasion!"

"Captain Widdershins," Violet said, "let's try to stick to the subject of the sugar bowl." She did not add that she was not interested in getting married for quite some time, particularly after Count Olaf had tried to marry her in one of his early schemes.

"Aye!" the captain cried. "Of course! Naturally! Aye! Tell us everything, Klaus! We'll eat while you talk! Aye! Sunny! Cookie! Serve the chowder!"

"Chowder is served!" announced Phil, as he hurried from the kitchen carrying two steaming bowls of thick soup. The youngest Baudelaire trailed behind him. Sunny was still a bit too young to carry hot food by herself, but she had found a pepper grinder, and circled the table offering fresh ground pepper to anyone who wanted some.

"Double pepper for me, Sunny!" Captain Widdershins cried, snatching the first bowl of chowder, although it is more polite to let one's guests be served first. "A nice hot bowl of chowder! A double helping of pepper! The location of the sugar bowl! Aye! That'll blow the barnacles off me! Aye! I'm so glad I scooped you Baudelaires out of the stream!"

"I'm glad, too," Fiona said, smiling shyly at Klaus.

"I couldn't be happier about it," Phil said, serving two more bowls of chowder. "I thought I'd never see you Baudelaires again, and here you are! All three of you have grown up so nicely, even though you've been constantly pursued by an evil villain and falsely accused of numerous crimes!"

"You certainly have had a harrowing journey," Fiona said, using a word which here means "frantic and extremely distressing."

"I'm afraid we may have another harrowing journey ahead of us," Klaus said. "When Captain Widdershins was talking about the philosopher who said that all of life is just shadows in a cave, I realized at once what that oval must be."

"A philosopher?" the captain asked. "That's impossible! Aye!"

"Absurdio," Sunny said, which meant "Philosophers live at the tops of mountains or in ivory towers, not underneath the sea."

"I think Klaus means a cave," Violet said quickly, rather than translating. "The oval must mark the entrance to a cave."

"It begins right near Anwhistle Aquatics," Klaus said, pointing to the chart. "The currents of the ocean would have brought the sugar bowl right to the entrance, and then the currents of the cave would have carried it far inside."

"But the chart only shows the entrance to the cave," Violet said. "We don't know what it's like inside. I wish Quigley was here. With his knowledge of maps, he might know the path of the cave."

"But Quigley isn't here," Klaus said gently. "I guess we'll be traveling in uncharted waters."

"That'll be fun," Phil said.

The Baudelaires looked at one another. The phrase "uncharted waters" does not only refer to underground locations that do not appear on charts. It is a phrase that can describe any place that is unknown, such as a forest in which every explorer has been lost, or one's own future, which cannot be known until it arrives. You don't have to be an optimist, like Phil, to find uncharted waters fun. I myself have spent many an enjoyable afternoon exploring the uncharted waters of a book I have not read, or a hiding place I discovered in a sideboard, a word which here means "a piece of furniture in the dining room, with shelves and drawers to hold various useful items." But the Baudelaires had already spent a great deal of time exploring uncharted waters, from the uncharted waters of Lake Lachrymose and its terrifying creatures, to the uncharted waters of secrets found in the Library of Records at Heimlich Hospital, to the uncharted waters of Count Olaf's wickedness, which were deeper and darker than any waters of the sea. After all of their uncharted traveling, the Baudelaire orphans were not in the mood to explore any uncharted waters, and could not share Phil's optimistic enthusiasm.

"It won't be the first time the *Queequeg*'s been in uncharted waters," Captain Widdershins said. "Aye—most of this sea was first explored by V.F.D. submarines."

"We thought V.F.D. stood for Volunteer Fire Department," Violet said. "Why would a fire department spend so much time underwater?"

"V.F.D. isn't just a fire department," the captain said, but his voice was very quiet, as if he were talking more to himself than to his crew. "Aye—it started that way. But the volunteers were interested in every such thing! I was one of the first to sign up for Voluntary Fish Domestication. That was one of the missions of Anwhistle Aquatics. Aye! I spent four long years training salmon to swim upstream and search for forest fires. That was when you were very young,

Fiona, but your brother worked right alongside me. You should have seen him sneaking extra worms to his favorites! Aye! The program was a modest success! Aye! But then Café Salmonella came along, and took our entire fleet away. The Snicket siblings fought as best they could. Aye! Historians call it the Snicket Snickersnee! Aye! But as the poet wrote, 'Too many waiters turn out to be traitors.'"

"The Snicket siblings?" Klaus was quick to ask.

"Aye," the captain said. "Three of them, each as noble as the next. Aye! Kit Snicket helped build this submarine! Aye! Jacques Snicket proved that the Royal Gardens Fire was arson! Aye! And the third sibling, with the marmosets—"

"You Baudelaires knew Jacques Snicket, didn't you?" asked Fiona, who wasn't shy about interrupting her stepfather.

"Very briefly," Violet said, "and we recently

found a message addressed to him. That's how we found about Thursday's gathering, at the last safe place."

"Nobody would write a message to Jacques," Captain Widdershins said. "Aye! Jacques is dead!"

"Etartsigam!" Sunny said, and her siblings quickly explained that she meant "The initials were J.S."

"It must be some other J.S.," Fiona said.

"Speaking of mysterious initials," Klaus said, "I wonder what G.G. stands for. If we knew what the cave was called, we might have a better idea of our journey."

"Aye!" Captain Widdershins said. "Let's guess! Great Glen! Aye! Green Glade! Aye! Glamorous Glacier! Aye! Gleeful Gameroom! Aye! Glass Goulash! Aye! Gothic Government! Aye! Grandma's Gingivitis! Aye! Girl Getting-up-from-table! Aye!"

Indeed, the captain's stepdaughter had stood up, wiped her mouth with a napkin embroidered with a portrait of Herman Melville, and walked over to a sideboard tucked into a far corner. Fiona opened a cabinet and revealed a few shelves stuffed with books. "Yesterday I started reading a new addition to my mycological library," she said, standing on tiptoes to reach the shelf. "I just remembered reading something that might come in handy."

The captain fingered his mustache in astonishment. "You and your mushrooms and molds!" the captain said. "I thought I'd never live to see your mycological studies be put to good use," and I'm sorry to say he was right.

"Let's see," Fiona said, paging through a thick book entitled *Mushroom Minutiae*, a word which here means "obscure facts." "It was in the table of contents—that's all I've read so far. It was about halfway through." She brought the book over to the table, and ran a finger down the table of contents while the Baudelaires leaned over to see. "Chapter Thirty-Six, The Yeast of Beasts. Chapter Thirty-Seven, Morel

Behavior in a Free Society. Chapter Thirty-Eight, Fungible Mold, Moldable Fungi. Chapter Thirty-Nine, Visitable Fungal Ditches. Chapter Forty, The Gorgonian Grotto—there!"

"Grotto?" Sunny asked.

"'Grotto' is another word for 'cave,'" Klaus explained, as Fiona flipped ahead to Chapter Forty.

"'The Gorgonian Grotto,'" she read, "'located in propinquity to Anwhistle Aquatics, has appropriately wraithlike nomenclature, with roots in Grecian mythology, as this conical cavern is fecund with what is perhaps the bugaboo of the entire mycological pantheon.'"

"Aye! I told you that book was too difficult!" Captain Widdershins said. "A young child can't unlock that sort of vocabulary."

"It's a very complicated prose style," Klaus admitted, "but I think I know what it says. The Gorgonian Grotto was named after something in Greek mythology."

"A Gorgon," Violet said. "Like that woman

with snakes instead of hair."

"She could turn people into stone," Fiona said.

"She was probably nice, when you got to know her," Phil said.

"Aye! I think I went to school with such a woman!" the captain said.

"I don't think she was a real person," Klaus said. "I think she was legendary. The book says it's appropriate that the grotto is named after a legendary monster, because there's a sort of monster living in a cave—a bugaboo."

"Bugaboo?" Sunny asked.

"A bugaboo can be any kind of monster," Klaus said. "We could call Count Olaf a bugaboo, if we felt so inclined."

"I'd rather not speak of him at all," Violet said.

"This bugaboo is a fungus of some sort," Fiona said, and continued reading from *Mushroom Minutiae*. "'The Medusoid Mycelium has a unique conducive strategy of waxing and waning: first a brief dormant cycle, in which the mycelium is nearly invisible, and then a precipitated flowering into speckled stalks and caps of such intense venom that it is fortunate the grotto serves as quarantine.'"

"I didn't understand all of that scientific terminology," Klaus said.

"I did," Fiona said. "There are three main parts to a mushroom. One is the cap, which is shaped like an umbrella, and the second is the stalk, which holds the umbrella up. Those are the parts you can see."

"There's part of a mushroom you can't see?" Violet asked.

"It's called the mycelium," Fiona replied. "It's like a bunch of thread, branching out underneath the ground. Some mushrooms have mycelia that go on for miles."

"How do you spell 'mycelium'?" Klaus asked, reaching into his waterproof pocket. "I want to write this down in my commonplace book."

Fiona pointed the word out on the page.

"The Medusoid Mycelium waxes and wanes," she said, "which means that the caps and stalks spring up from the mycelium, and then wither away, and then spring up again. It sounds like you wouldn't know the mushrooms are there until they poke up out of the ground."

The Baudelaires pictured a group of mushrooms suddenly springing up under their feet, and felt a bit queasy, as if they already knew of the dreadful encounter they would soon have with this terrible fungus. "That sounds unnerving," Violet said.

"It gets worse," Fiona said. "The mushrooms are exceedingly poisonous. Listen to this: 'As the poet says, *"A single spore has such grim power/That you may die within the hour."*'" A spore is like a seed—if it has a place to grow, it will become another mycelium. But if someone eats it, or even breathes it in, it can cause death."

"Within the hour?" Klaus said. "That's a fast-acting poison."

"Most fungal poisons have cures," Fiona

said. "The poison of a deadly fungus can be the source of some wonderful medicines. I've been working on a few myself. But this book says it's lucky the grotto acts as quarantine."

"Quarwa?" Sunny asked.

"Quarantine is when something dangerous is isolated, so the danger cannot spread," Klaus explained. "Because the Medusoid Mycelium is in uncharted waters, very few people have been poisoned. If someone brought even one spore to dry land, who knows what would happen?"

"We won't find out!" Captain Widdershins said. "We're not going to take any spores! Aye! We're just going to grab the sugar bowl and be on our way! Aye! I'll set a course right now!"

The captain bounded up from the table and began climbing the rope ladder to the *Queequeg*'s controls. "Are you sure we should continue our mission?" Fiona asked her stepfather, shutting the book. "It sounds very dangerous."

"Dangerous? Aye! Dangerous and scary! Aye! Scary and difficult! Aye! Difficult and mysterious! Aye! Mysterious and uncomfortable! Aye! Uncomfortable and risky! Aye! Risky and noble! Aye!"

"I suppose the fungus can't hurt us if we're inside the submarine," Phil said, struggling to remain optimistic.

"Even if it could!" the captain cried, standing at the top of the rope ladder and gesturing dramatically as he delivered an impassioned oratory, a phrase which here means "emotional speech that the Baudelaires found utterly convincing, even if they did not quite agree with every word." "The amount of treachery in this world is enormous!" he cried. "Aye! Think of the crafts we saw on the sonar screen! Think of Count Olaf's enormous submarine, and the even more enormous one that chased it away! Aye! There's always something more enormous and more terrifying on our tails! Aye! And so many of the noble submarines are gone! Aye! You think the Herman Melville suits are the only noble uniforms in the world? There used to be volunteers with P. G. Wodehouse on their uniforms, and Carl Van Vechten. There was Comyns and Cleary and Archy and Mehitabel. But now volunteers are scarce! So the best we can do is one small noble thing! Aye! Like retrieving the sugar bowl from the Gorgonian Grotto, no matter how grim it sounds! Aye! Remember my personal philosophy! He who hesitates is lost!"

"Or she!" Fiona said.

"Or she," the captain agreed. "Aye?"

"Aye!" Violet cried.

"Aye!" Klaus shouted.

"Aye!" Sunny shrieked.

"Hooray!" Phil yelled.

Captain Widdershins peered down in annoyance at Phil, whom he would have preferred say "Aye!" along with everyone else. "Cookie!" he ordered. "Do the dishes! The rest of you get some shut-eye! Aye!"

"Shut-eye?" Violet asked.

"Aye! It means 'sleep'!" the captain explained.

"We know what it means," Klaus said. "We're just surprised that we're supposed to sleep through the mission."

"It'll take some time to get to the cave!" the captain said. "I want you four to be well-rested in case you're needed! Now go to your barracks! Aye!"

It is one of life's bitterest truths that bedtime so often arrives just when things are really getting interesting. The Baudelaires were not particularly in the mood to toss and turn in the *Queequeg*'s barracks—a word which here means "a type of bedroom that is usually uncomfortable"—as the submarine drew closer and closer to the mysterious grotto and its indispensible item, a phrase which here means "the sugar bowl, although the children did not know why it was so important." But as they followed Fiona out of the Main Hall and back down the corridor, past the plaque advertising the captain's personal philosophy, the door to the supply room, and an uncountable number of leaky metal pipes, the siblings felt quite tired, and by the time Fiona opened a door to reveal a small, green-lit room stacked with saggy bunk beds, the three children were already yawning. Perhaps it was because of their long, exhausting day, which had begun on the icy summit of Mount Fraught, but Violet didn't ponder one single mechanical idea as she got into bed, as she usually did before she went to sleep. Klaus scarcely had time to put his glasses on a small bedside table before he nodded off, a phrase which here means "fell asleep without considering even one of the books he had recently read." Sunny curled up on a pillow, and she didn't waste one moment dreaming up new recipes—preferably entrées that were less mushy than chowder, as she still enjoyed biting things as much as she did when she was a baby—

before she was dreaming herself. And even Fiona, whose bedtime habits are less familiar to me than that of the Baudelaires', put her glasses next to Klaus's and was asleep in moments. The whirring engine of the *Queequeg* sent them deeper and deeper into slumber for several hours, and they probably would have slept much longer if the children hadn't been awakened by a terrible—and terribly familiar—noise. It was a loud, unnerving scraping, like fingernails against a chalkboard, and the Baudelaires were almost shaken out of bed as the entire submarine rattled.

"What was that?" Violet asked.

"We hit something," Fiona said grimly, grabbing her glasses in one hand and her diving helmet in the other. "We'd better see what the situation is."

The Baudelaires nodded in agreement, and hurried out of the barracks and back down the corridor. There was an unnerving splashing

sound coming from a few of the tubes, and
Klaus had to pick up Sunny to carry her over
several large puddles.

"Is the submarine collapsing?" Klaus asked.

"We'll know soon enough," Fiona said, and
she was correct. In moments she'd led the Baudelaires back into the Main Hall, where Phil and the
captain were standing at the table, staring out the
porthole into black nothingness. They each had
grim expressions on their faces, although Phil was
trying to smile at the same time.

"It's good you got some rest," the optimist
said. "There's a real adventure ahead of you."

"I'm glad you brought your diving helmets,"
Captain Widdershins said. "Aye!"

"Why?" Violet asked. "Is the *Queequeg* seriously damaged?"

"Aye!" the captain said. "I mean, no. The
submarine is damaged, but she'll hold—for now.
We reached the Gorgonian Grotto about an hour
ago, and I was able to steer us inside with no
problem. But the cave got narrower and narrower

as we maneuvered further and further inside."

"The book said the grotto was conical," Klaus said. "That means it's shaped like a cone."

"Aye!" the captain said. "The entrance was the wide end of the cone, but now it's too narrow for the submarine to travel. If we want to retrieve the sugar bowl we'll have to use something smaller."

"Periscope?" Sunny asked.

"No," Captain Widdershins replied. "A child."

CHAPTER Six

"*You* youngsters look very spiffy in those helmets!" Phil said, with a wide, optimistic smile on his face. "I know you must be a little nervous, but I'm sure all of you children will rise to the occasion!"

The Baudelaire orphans sighed, and looked at one another from inside their diving helmets. When someone tells you that you will rise to the occasion, it means they think you'll be strong or skillful enough for a particular situation, but Violet, Klaus, and Sunny did not know if they could rise to the occasion when they were so afraid of sinking. Although they had dragged their helmets back and forth to the barracks, they hadn't realized how awkward they were until they had strapped them onto their waterproof uniforms. Violet did not like the fact that she couldn't reach through the helmet to tie up her hair, in case she needed to invent something on the spur of the moment, a phrase which here means "while traveling through the Gorgonian Grotto." Klaus found that it was difficult to see, as the small circular window in his helmet interfered with his glasses. And Sunny was not at all happy about curling up inside her helmet, shutting the tiny door, and being carried by her sister as if she were a volleyball instead of a young girl. When they had put their uniforms on just a few hours earlier, the three siblings thought that the waterproof suits had fit them like a glove. But now, as they followed Captain

Widdershins out of the Main Hall and down the damp and dripping corridor, the children feared that the uniforms fit more like an anchor, dragging them down to the depths of the sea.

"Don't worry," Fiona said, as though she were reading the Baudelaires' minds. She gave the siblings a small smile from behind her diving helmet. "I assure you that these suits are completely safe—safe, but uncomfortable."

"As long as we can breathe," Violet said, "I don't care how uncomfortable they are."

"Of course you'll be able to breathe!" the captain said. "Aye! The oxygen systems in your helmets provide plenty of air for a short journey! Of course, if there's any opportunity to remove your helmets, you should do so! Aye! That way the system can recharge itself, and you'll have more air."

"Where would we find an opportunity to remove our helmets in an underwater cave?" Klaus asked.

"Who knows?" Captain Widdershins said. "Aye! You'll be in uncharted waters. I wish I could go myself! Aye! But the grotto has become too narrow!"

"Hewenkella," Sunny said. Her voice was muffled inside the helmet, and it was difficult for even her siblings to know what she was saying.

"I think my sister is curious about how we'll be able to see our way," Violet said. "Does the *Queequeg* have any waterproof flashlights?"

"Flashlights won't help you," the captain replied. "Aye! It's too dark! Aye! But you won't need to see your way. Aye! If Klaus's calculations are correct, the tide will just push you along. Aye! You won't even have to swim! You can just sit there, and you'll drift right to the sugar bowl!"

"That seems like an awfully passive way to travel," Fiona said.

"Aye!" her stepfather agreed. "It does! But there is no other solution! And we should not hesitate!" He stopped and pointed to his plaque.

"He or she who hesitates is lost!" he reminded them.

"It's a little hard not to hesitate," Violet said, "before doing something like this."

"It's not too late to draw straws!" the captain said. "Aye! You don't all have to go together!"

"The three of us prefer not to be separated," Klaus said. "We've had too much trouble that way."

"I should think you've had too much trouble in any case!" the captain said. "Aye!"

"The Baudelaires are right, Stepfather," Fiona said. "This way makes the most sense. We may need Violet's mechanical expertise, or Klaus's knowledge of the tidal charts. And Sunny's size may come in handy, if the grotto gets even smaller."

"Ulp," Sunny said, which meant something like, "I don't like the idea of drifting by myself in a diving helmet."

"What about you, Fiona?" the captain asked. "Aye! You could stay here with me!"

"My skills might be needed as well," Fiona said quietly, and the Baudelaires shuddered, trying not to think about the Medusoid Mycelium and its poisonous spores.

"Aye!" Captain Widdershins admitted, and smoothed his mustache with one gloved finger. "Well, I'm going to tell V.F.D. all about this! Aye! All four of you volunteers will receive citations for bravery!"

The Baudelaires looked at one another as best they could through the small circular windows. A citation for bravery is nothing more than a piece of paper stating that you have been courageous at some time, and such citations have not been known to be very useful when confronted by danger, whether deep underwater, or, as the Baudelaires would eventually learn, high up in the air. Anyone can write up a citation for bravery, and I have even been known to write one for myself from time to time, in order to keep my spirits up in the middle of a treacherous journey. The three siblings were more interested in surviving their voyage through the Gorgonian Grotto than in receiving a written statement complimenting them on their courage, but they knew Captain Widdershins was trying to keep their spirits up as he led them down the corridor and into the room where they had first encountered the captain of the *Queequeg.*

"To get into the water," the captain said, "you just climb up that same ladder and give a holler when you're at the hatch. Then I'll activate a valve down here, so the submarine won't flood with water when you open it. Then, as I said, you'll just let the current carry you. You should end up in the same place as the sugar bowl."

"And you still won't tell us why the sugar bowl is important?" Violet couldn't help asking.

"It's not the sugar bowl," Captain Widdershins said, "it's what's inside it. Aye! I've already said too much! Aye! There are secrets in this world too terrible for young people to know!

Just think—if you knew about the sugar bowl and you somehow fell into Count Olaf's clutches, there's no telling what he'd do! Aye!"

"But look on the bright side," Phil pointed out. "Whatever terrible things may be lurking in that cave, you won't find Count Olaf. There's no way that octopus submarine could fit!"

"Aye!" the captain agreed. "But we'll watch for him on the sonar, just in case! We'll watch you too! Aye! We'll be right here watching you the entire time! The oxygen systems in your helmets make enough noise that you'll appear as four tiny dots on our screen! Now, off you go! Good luck!"

"We'll be wishing you the best!" Phil said.

The adults gave each of the children a pat on the helmet, and without any further hesitation, off went the Baudelaire children with Fiona behind them, following the ladder up to the hatch through which they had come aboard. The four volunteers were quiet as they made their way up, until Violet reached up with one hand—the other hand was clutching Sunny's helmet—and grabbed the handle that opened the hatch.

"We're ready!" she called down, although she did not feel ready at all.

"Aye!" replied the voice of the captain. "I'm activating the valve now! Wait five seconds and then open the hatch! Aye! But don't hesitate! Aye! He who hesitates is lost! Aye! Or she! Aye! Good luck! Aye! Good fortune! Aye! Good journey! Aye! Good-bye!"

There was a distant clanging, presumably the sound of the valve activating, and the four children waited for five seconds, just as you may wish to wait a few seconds yourself, so all thoughts of the Baudelaires' predicament will vanish from your imagination so that you will not be weeping as you learn several boring facts about the water cycle. The water cycle, to review, consists of three key phenomena—evaporation, precipitation, and collection—which are all equally boring and thus equally less upsetting than what happened to the Baudelaires when Violet opened the hatch and the icy, dark waters of the sea rushed into the passageway. If you were to read what happened to them in the moments that followed, you would find yourself unable to sleep as you wept into your pillow and pictured the children all alone in that grim grotto, drifting slowly to the end of the cavern, and yet if you read about the water cycle you would find yourself unable to stay awake, due to the boring description of the process by which water is distributed around the world, and so as a courtesy to you I will continue this book in a way that is best for all concerned.

The water cycle consists of three phenomena—evaporation, precipitation, and collection—which are the three phenomena that make up what is known as "the water cycle." Evaporation, the first of these phenomena, is the process of water turning into vapor and eventually forming clouds, such as those found in cloudy skies, or on cloudy days, or even cloudy nights. These clouds are formed by a phenomenon known as "evaporation," which is the first of three phenomena that make up the water cycle. Evaporation, the first of these three, is simply a term for a process by which water turns into vapor and eventually forms clouds. Clouds can be recognized by their appearance, usually on cloudy days or nights, when they can be seen in cloudy skies. The name for the process by which clouds are formed—by water, which turns into vapor and becomes part of the formation known as "clouds"—is "evaporation," the first phenomenon in the three phenomena that make up the cycle of water, otherwise known as "the water cycle," and surely you must be asleep by now and so can be spared the horrifying details of the Baudelaires' journey.

The instant Violet opened the hatch, the passageway flooded with water, and the children drifted out of the submarine and into the blackness of the Gorgonian Grotto. The Baudelaires knew, of course, that the *Queequeg* had entered an underwater cave, but still they were unprepared for how very dark and cold it was. Sunlight had not reached the waters of the grotto for quite some time—not since Anwhistle Aquatics was still up and running, a phrase which here means "not destroyed under suspicious circumstances"—and the water felt like a freezing black glove, encircling the children with its chilly fingers. As Klaus had predicted after studying the tidal charts, the currents of the cave carried the youngsters away from the submarine, but in the darkness it was impossible to see how fast or far they were going. Within moments the four volunteers lost sight of the *Queequeg*, and then of one another. Had the grotto been equipped with some sort of lighting system, as it once had, the children could have seen a number of things. They might have noticed the mosaic on the grotto floor—thousands and thousands of colorful tiles, depicting noble events from the early history of a secret organization, and portraits of famous

writers, scientists, artists, musicians, philosophers, and chefs who had inspired the organization's members. They might have seen an
enormous, rusted pumping machine, which was
able to drain the entire grotto, or flood it with
seawater again, in mere minutes. They might
have gazed upward and seen the sharp angles
of various Vertical Flame Diversions and other
secret passageways that once led all the way up
to the marine research center and rhetorical
advice service, or even spotted the person who
was using one of the passageways now, and
probably for the last time, as she made her difficult and dark way toward the *Queequeg*. But
instead, all the children could see through their
small circular windows was darkness. The
Baudelaires had seen darkness before, of
course—darkness in secret passageways and
tunnels, darkness in abandoned buildings and
empty streets, darkness in the eyes of wicked
people, and even darkness in other caves. But
never before had the orphans felt so completely

in the dark as they did now. They did not know
where they were, although once Violet felt, very
briefly, her feet brush up against something very
smooth, like a tile fitted firmly against the
ground. They could not tell where they were
going, although after a while Klaus had a suspi-
cion that the current had spun him so he was
traveling upside down. And they could not tell
when they would arrive, although from time to
time Sunny saw, through her diving helmet, a
tiny dot of light, much like the tiny dots Captain Widdershins said they would appear as on
the sonar screen of his submarine.

The Baudelaires drifted along in cold, dark
silence, feeling afraid and confused and
strangely lonely, and when their journey finally
ended, it was so sudden it felt as if they had
fallen into a deep, deep sleep, as deep and dark
as the cavern itself, and now were being jolted
awake. At first, it sounded as if a bushel of broken glass were raining down on the children,
but then the children realized they had drifted

to the surface of the water, and in one curling, fluid motion, the tide pushed them onto something that felt like a beach, and the three siblings found themselves crawling on a slope of dark, wet sand.

"Klaus?" Violet called through her helmet. "Are you there? What's happened?"

"I don't know," Klaus replied. He could just barely see his sister crawling alongside him. "We couldn't have reached the surface of the sea— we were very, very deep. Is Sunny with you?"

"Yes," Sunny said, from inside her helmet. "Fiona?"

"I'm here," came the voice of the mycologist. "But where are we? How can we still be below the surface of the sea, without any water around us?"

"I'm not sure," Klaus said, "but it must be possible. After all, a submarine can be below the sea and stay dry."

"Are we on another submarine?" Violet asked.

"I dunno," Sunny said, and frowned in her helmet. "Look!"

The elder Baudelaires looked, although it took them a few moments to realize what Sunny was talking about, as they could not see what direction their sister was pointing. But in a moment they saw two small lights, a short distance from where the volunteers were crawling. Hesitantly, they stood up—except for Sunny, who remained curled up in her helmet—and saw that the lights were coming from a place many lights come from: lamps. A short distance away, standing against the wall, were three floorlamps, each with a letter on its shade. The first lamp had a large V, and the second had an F. The third floorlamp had burnt out, and it was too dim to read the shade, but the children knew, of course, that it must have had a D.

"What is this place?" Fiona asked, but as the children stepped closer they could see what kind of place it was.

As they had suspected, the currents of the

Gorgonian Grotto had carried them to a beach, but it was a beach contained in a narrow room. The youngsters stood at the top of the slope of sand and peered at this small, dim room, with smooth tiled walls that looked damp and slippery, and a sand floor covered in an assortment of small objects, some in piles and some half-buried in the sand. The children could see bottles, some still with their corks and caps, and some cans still intact from their journey. There were a few books, their pages bloated as if soaked in water, and a few small cases that looked locked. There was a roller skate, turned upside down, and a deck of cards sitting in two piles, as if someone were about to shuffle them. Here and there were a few pens, sticking out of the sand like porcupine quills, and there were many more objects the children could not identify in the gloom.

"Where are we?" Fiona asked. "Why isn't this place full of water?"

Klaus looked up, but could not see past a

few feet. "This must be a passage of some sort," Klaus said, "straight up to dry land—an island, maybe, or maybe it curves to the shore."

"Anwhistle Aquatics," Violet said thoughtfully. "We must be underneath its ruins."

"Oxo?" Sunny asked, which meant "Does that mean we can breathe without our helmets?"

"I think so," Klaus said, and then carefully removed his helmet, an action for which I would have given him a citation for bravery. "Yes," he said. "We can breathe. Everybody take off their helmets—that way, our oxygen systems will recharge."

"But what is this place?" Fiona asked again, removing her helmet. "Why would anybody build a room way down here?"

"It looks like it's been abandoned," Violet said. "It's full of junk."

"Someone must come to change the lightbulbs," Klaus pointed out. "Besides, all this junk was washed up here by the tide, like us."

"And like sugar bowl," Sunny said.

"Of course," Fiona said, looking down at the objects in the sand. "It must be here someplace."

"Let's find it and get out of here," Violet said. "I don't like this place."

"Mission," Sunny said, which meant "Once we find the sugar bowl, our work here is done."

"Not quite," Klaus said. "We'll still have to return to the *Queequeg*—against the current, I might add. Looking for the sugar bowl is only half the battle."

Everyone nodded in agreement, and the four volunteers spread out and began to examine the objects in the sand. Saying that something is half the battle is like saying something is half a sandwich, because it is dangerous to announce that something is half the battle when the much more difficult part might still be waiting in the wings, a phrase which here means "coming up more quickly than you'd like." You might think learning how to boil water is half the battle, only to learn that making a poached egg is much trickier than you thought. You might think that climbing a mountain is half the battle, only to find out that the mountain goats who live at the top are vicious, and heavily armed. And you might think that rescuing a kidnapped ichnologist is half the battle, only to discover that making a poached egg is much trickier than you thought and that the entire battle would be much more difficult and dangerous than you ever would have imagined. The Baudelaires and their mycologist friend thought that looking for the sugar bowl was half the battle, but I'm sorry to tell you that they were wrong, and it is lucky that you fell asleep earlier, during my description of the water cycle, so you will not learn about the other half of the Baudelaires' battle, and the ghastly poison they would end up battling not long after their search through the sand.

"I've found a box of rubber bands," Violet said, after a few minutes, "and a doorknob, two mattress springs, half a bottle of vinegar, and a paring knife, but no sugar bowl."

"I've found an earring, a broken clipboard, a book of poetry, half a stapler, and three swizzle sticks," Klaus said, "but no sugar bowl."

"Three can soup," Sunny said, "jar peanut butter, box crackers, pesto, wasabi, lo mein. But nadasuchre."

"This is harder than I thought," Klaus said. "What have you found, Fiona?"

Fiona did not answer.

"Fiona?" Klaus asked again, and the Baudelaires turned to look at her. But the mycologist was not looking at the siblings. She was looking past them, and her eyes were wide with fear behind her triangular glasses. "Fiona?" Klaus said, sounding a bit worried. "What have you found?"

Fiona swallowed, and pointed back down at the slope of sand. "Mycelium," she said finally, in a faint whisper, and the Baudelaires turned to see that she had spoken the truth. Sprouting

out of the sand, quickly and silently, were the stalks and caps of the Medusoid Mycelium, the fungus Fiona had described back on the *Queequeg*. The invisible threads of the mycelium, according to her mycological book, waxed and waned, and had been waning when the volunteers drifted ashore, which meant that the mushrooms had been hiding underground when the children had arrived at this strange room. But now, as time passed, they were waxing, and sprouting up all over the beach and even along the smooth, tiled walls. At first just a handful were visible—each one a dark, gray color, with black splotches on the caps as if they were spattered with ink—and then more and more, like a silent, deadly crowd that had gathered on the beach and was staring blindly at the terrified children. The mushrooms only ventured halfway up the slope of sand, so it seemed that the poisonous fungus was not going to engulf them—not yet, anyway. But as the mycelium continued to wax, the entire beach sprouted in sinister mushrooms, and until it waned the Baudelaires had to huddle on the sand, in the light of the floorlamps, and stare back at the venomous mycological crowd. More and more mushrooms appeared, crowding the strange shore and piling up on top of one another as if they were pushing and shoving to get a good look at the trapped and frightened children. Looking for the sugar bowl may have been half the battle, but now the Baudelaire orphans were trapped, and that half was much, much more troubling.

The word "lousy," like the word "volunteer,"
the word "fire," the word "department," and
many other words found in dictionaries and
other important documents, has a number of
different definitions depending on the exact circumstances in which it is used. There is the
common definition of the word "lousy," meaning "bad," and this definition of "lousy" has
described many things in my history of the
Baudelaire orphans, from the sinister smells of
Lousy Lane, along which the children traveled

long ago, to their lousy journey up and down the Mortmain Mountains in search of the V.F.D. headquarters. There is the medical definition of the word "lousy," meaning "infested with lice," and this definition of "lousy" has not appeared in my work at all, although as Count Olaf's hygiene gets worse and worse I may find occasion to use it. And then there is a somewhat obscure definition of the word "lousy," meaning "abundantly supplied," the way Count Olaf is lousy with treacherous plans, or the *Queequeg* is lousy with metal pipes, or the entire world is lousy with unfathomable secrets, and it is this definition that the Baudelaire orphans pondered, as they huddled with Fiona underneath the mysterious floorlamps of the Gorgonian Grotto, and watched more and more mushrooms sprout from the sand. As their surroundings became lousy with the Medusoid Mycelium, the children thought of all the other things in their lives with which they were abundantly supplied. The children's lives were lousy with mystery, from the mysteries of V.F.D. to the mysteries of their own futures, with each mystery crowding the others like the stalks and caps of the poisonous fungi. Their lives were lousy with danger, from the dangers they had encountered above mountains and underneath buildings, to the dangers they had faced inside the city and out in the hinterlands, from the dangers of villainous people to the dangers of kind people who did not know any better. And their lives were lousy with lousiness, from terrible people to horrible meals, from terrifying locations to horrifying circumstances, and from dreadful inconveniences to inconvenient dreads, so that it seemed that their lives would always be lousy, lousy with lousy days and lousy with lousy nights, even if all of the lousy things with which their lives were lousy became less lousy, and less lousy with lousiness, over the lousy course of each lousy-with-lousiness moment, and with each new lousy mushroom, making the cave lousier and lousier with lousiness, it was almost too much for the Baudelaire orphans to bear.

"Lousy," Sunny said.

"This is not good news," Klaus agreed. "Fiona, do you think we've been poisoned already?"

"No," Fiona said firmly. "The spores shouldn't reach us here. As long as we stay here at the far end of the cavern, and the mushrooms don't advance any further, we should be safe."

"It looks like they've stopped advancing," Violet said, pointing at the line of gray mushrooms, and the other volunteers saw that she was right. There were still new mushrooms popping up, but the fungus didn't seem to be getting any closer to the four children.

"I guess the mycelium has only grown that far," Fiona said. "We're very lucky."

"I don't feel very lucky," Klaus said. "I feel trapped. How will we get out of here?"

"There's only one way," Violet said. "The

only path back to the *Queequeg* leads through those mushrooms."

"If we go through the mushrooms," Fiona said, "we'll most likely be poisoned. One spore could easily slip through our suits."

"Antidote?" Sunny asked.

"I might find the recipe for a cure," Fiona replied, "someplace in my mycological library. But we don't want to take that chance. We'll have to exit another way."

For a moment, all four children looked up, into the blackness of the passage above their heads. Violet frowned, and put one hand on the damp and slippery tiles of the wall. With the other hand she reached into the waterproof pocket of her uniform, and drew out a ribbon to tie up her hair.

"Can we go out that way?" Klaus asked. "Can you invent something to help us climb up that passageway?"

"Tingamebob," Sunny said, which meant "There's plenty of materials here in the sand."

"Materials aren't the problem," Violet said, and peered up into the blackness. "We're far below the surface of the water. It must be miles and miles to the surface. Even the best climbing device would wear out over the journey, and if it did we'd fall all the way down."

"But someone must use that passageway," Klaus said. "Otherwise it wouldn't have been built."

"It doesn't matter," Fiona said. "We can't go out that way. We need to get to the *Queequeg*. Otherwise, my stepfather will wonder what's become of us. Eventually he'd put on his diving helmet and go investigate . . ."

"And the tide would carry him right into the poisonous fungus," Klaus finished. "Fiona's right. Even if we could climb all the way up, it'd be the wrong way to go."

"But what else can we do?" Violet said, her voice rising. "We can't spend the rest of our lives in this miserable place!"

Fiona looked at the mushrooms and sighed.

"*Mushroom Minutiae* said that this fungus waxes and wanes. Right now it's waxing. We'll have to wait until it wanes again, and then run quickly over the sand and swim back down to the submarine."

"But how long will it be until it starts waning?" Klaus said.

"I don't know," Fiona admitted. "It could be just a few minutes, or a few hours. It could even be a few days."

"A few days?" Violet said. "In a few days your stepfather will give up on us! In a few days we'll miss the V.F.D. gathering! We can't wait a few days!"

"It's our only choice," Klaus said, putting a comforting hand on Violet's shoulder. "We can wait until the mushrooms disappear, or we can find ourselves poisoned."

"That's not a choice at all," Violet replied bitterly.

"It's a Hobson's choice," Klaus said. "Remember?"

The eldest Baudelaire looked down at her brother and gave him a small smile. "Of course I remember," she said.

"Mamasan," Sunny said. Her siblings looked down at her, and Violet picked her up in her arms.

"Who's Hobson?" Fiona asked. "What was his choice?"

Klaus smiled. "Thomas Hobson lived in Britain in the seventeenth century," he said. "He was in charge of a stable, and according to legend, he always told his customers they had a choice: they could take the horse closest to the door, or no horse at all."

"That's not really a choice," Fiona said.

Violet smiled. "Precisely," she said. "A Hobson's choice is something that's not a choice at all. It's an expression our mother used to use. She'd say, 'I'll give you a Hobson's choice, Violet—you can clean your room or I will stand in the doorway and sing your least favorite song over and over.'"

Fiona grinned. "What was your least favorite song?" she asked.

"'Row, Row, Row Your Boat,'" Violet said. "I hate the part about life being but a dream."

"She'd offer me the Hobson's choice of doing the dishes or reading the poetry of Edgar Guest," Klaus said. "He's my absolute least favorite poet."

"Bath or pink dress," Sunny said.

"Did your mother always joke around like that?" Fiona asked. "Mine used to get awfully mad if I didn't clean my room."

"Our mother would get mad, too," Klaus said. "Remember, Violet, when we left the window of the library open, and that night it rained?"

"She really flew off the handle," Violet said, using a phrase which here means "became extremely angry." "We spoiled an atlas that she said was irreplaceable."

"You should have heard her yell," Klaus said. "Our father came down from his study to see what was the matter."

"And then he started yelling, too," Violet said, and the Baudelaires paused and looked at one another uncomfortably. Everyone yells, of course, from time to time, but the Baudelaire children did not like to think about their parents yelling, particularly now that they were no longer around to apologize or explain themselves. It is often difficult to admit that someone you love is not perfect, or to consider aspects of a person that are less than admirable. To the Baudelaires it felt almost as if they had drawn a line after their parents died—a secret line in their memories, separating all the wonderful things about the Baudelaire parents from the things that perhaps were not quite so wonderful. Since the fire, whenever they thought of their parents, the Baudelaires never stepped over this secret line, preferring to ponder the best moments the family had together rather than any of the times when they had fought, or been unfair or selfish. But now, suddenly, in the gloom of the Gorgonian Grotto, the siblings had stumbled across that line and found themselves thinking of that angry afternoon in the library, and in moments other angry afternoons and evenings had occurred to them until their brains were lousy with memories of all stripes, a phrase which here means "both good and bad." It gave the siblings a queasy feeling to cross this line in their memories, and admit that their parents were sometimes difficult, and it made them feel all the queasier to realize they could not step back, and pretend they had never remembered these less-than-perfect moments, any more than they could step back in time, and once again find themselves safe in the Baudelaire home, before fire and Count Olaf had appeared in their lives.

"My brother used to get angry, too," Fiona said. "Before he disappeared, he would have awful fights with my stepfather—late at night, when they thought I was asleep."

"Your stepfather didn't mention that," Violet said. "He said your brother was a charming man."

"Maybe he only remembers the charming parts," Fiona replied. "Maybe he doesn't want to remember everything. Maybe he wants to keep those parts secret."

"Do you think your stepfather knew about this place?" Klaus asked, looking around the eerie room. "He mentioned that we might find a place to take off our diving helmets, remember? It seemed strange at the time."

"I don't know," Fiona said. "Maybe that's another secret he was keeping."

"Like the sugar bowl," Violet said.

"Speaking which," Sunny said.

"Sunny's right," Klaus said. "We should keep looking for the sugar bowl."

"It must be here someplace," Fiona agreed, "and besides, we need some way to pass the time until the fungus wanes. Everyone should spread out, and give a shout if you find the sugar bowl."

The Baudelaires nodded in agreement, and the four volunteers took distant positions on the sand, taking care not to step any closer to the Medusoid Mycelium. For the next few hours, they dug through the sand floor of the grotto and examined what they found by the light of the two floorlamps. Each layer of sand uncovered several items of interest, but no matter how many objects the children encountered, no one gave a shout. Violet found a butter dish, a length of electrical wire, and an odd, square stone with messages carved in three languages, but not what she was looking for, and so the eldest Baudelaire remained silent. Klaus found a box of toothpicks, a small hand puppet, and a ring made of dull metal, but not what he had come to the cave to find, and so the middle Baudelaire merely sighed. And Sunny found two cloth napkins, a broken telephone receiver, and a fancy wineglass filled with holes, but when she finally opened her mouth to speak, the youngest Baudelaire merely said, "Snack!" which meant something like, "Why don't we stop for a bite to eat?" and quickly opened the crackers and peanut butter she had found.

"Thanks, Sunny," Fiona said, taking a cracker spread with peanut butter. "I must say, Baudelaires, I'm getting frustrated. My hands ache from all that digging, but there's no sign of the sugar bowl."

"I'm beginning to think this is a fool's errand," Violet said, using a phrase which here means "errand performed by a fool." "We journeyed all the way down here to find a crucial item, and instead it seems like we're finding nothing but junk. It's a waste of time."

"Not necessarily," Klaus said, eating a cracker and looking at the items he had found. "We may not have found the sugar bowl, but I think we did find some crucial information."

"What do you mean?" Violet said.

"Look at this," Klaus said, and held up a book he had taken from the sand. "It's a collection of poetry, and most of it is too damp to read. But look at the title page."

The middle Baudelaire held open the book

so the other volunteers could see. *"Versed Furtive Disclosure,"* Violet read out loud.

"V.F.D.," Sunny said.

"Yes," Klaus said. "'Furtive' means 'secretive,' and 'disclosure' means 'to reveal something.' I think V.F.D. may have hidden things here—not just the sugar bowl, but other secrets."

"That would make sense," Violet said. "This grotto is a bit like a secret passageway—like the one we found underneath our home, or the one Quigley found underneath his."

Fiona nodded, and began to search through a pile of items she had taken from the sand. "I found an envelope earlier," she said, "but I didn't think to open it. I was too busy concentrating on the sugar bowl."

"Punctilio," Sunny said, holding up a torn and tattered sheet of newspaper. The children could see the letters "V.F.D." circled in a headline.

"I'm too exhausted to dig anymore," Violet said. "Let's spend some time reading instead.

Klaus, you can examine that poetry book. Fiona, you can see if there's anything worthwhile in that envelope. And I'll take a look at the clipping Sunny found."

"Me?" asked Sunny, whose reading skills were still developing.

"Why don't you cook us something, Sunny," Klaus suggested with a smile. "Those crackers just whetted my appetite."

"Pronto," the youngest Baudelaire promised, looking at the foodstuffs she had found in the sand, most of which were sealed up tight. The phrase "whet my appetite," as you probably know, refers to one's hunger being awakened, and usually it refers to food. The Baudelaires had lost track of time while searching through the sand of the grotto, and the snack Sunny prepared made them realize just how long it had been since they had eaten. But another appetite had been whetted for the Baudelaires as well—a hunger for secrets, and for information that might help them. As Sunny began to prepare a meal for her fellow volunteers, Violet and Klaus looked over the materials they had found, devouring whatever information seemed important, and Fiona did the same thing, leaning up against the tiled wall of the cavern as she examined the contents of the envelope she had found. The volunteers' hunger for information was almost as fierce as their hunger for food, and after a lengthy period of studying and note taking, whisking and mixing, the four children could not say whether they were more eager to hear about the others' research or to eat the meal Sunny had prepared.

"What is this?" Violet asked her sister, peering into the fishbowl Sunny was using as a serving dish.

"Pesto lo mein," Sunny explained.

"What my sister means," Klaus said, "is that she found a package of soft Chinese noodles, which she tossed with an Italian basil sauce she got out of a jar."

"That's quite an international combination," Fiona said.

"Hobson," Sunny said, which meant "I didn't have much choice, given our surroundings," and then held up another item she had found. "Wasabi?"

"What's wasabi?" Violet asked.

"It's a Japanese condiment," Klaus said. "It's very spicy, and often served with fish."

"Why don't we save the wasabi, Sunny," Violet said, taking the tin of wasabi and putting it in the pocket of her uniform. "We'll take it back to the *Queequeg* and you can use it in a seafood recipe."

Sunny nodded in agreement, and passed the fishbowl to her siblings. "Utensi," she said.

"We can use these swizzle sticks as chopsticks," Klaus said. "We'll have to take turns, and whoever isn't eating can tell us what they've discovered. Here, Fiona, why don't you go first?"

"Thanks," Fiona said, taking the swizzle sticks gratefully. "I'm quite hungry. Did you learn anything from that poetry book?"

"Not as much as I would have liked," Klaus said. "Most of the pages were soaked from their journey, and so I couldn't read much. But I believe I've learned a new code: Verse Fluctuation Declaration. It's a way to communicate by substituting words in poems."

"I don't understand," Violet said.

"It's a bit tricky," Klaus said, opening his commonplace book, in which he'd copied the information. "The book uses a poem called 'My Last Duchess,' by Robert Browning, as an example."

"I've read that," Fiona said, twirling a few noodles around a swizzle stick to get them into her mouth. "It's a very creepy story about a man who murders his wife."

"Right," Klaus said. "But if a volunteer used the name of the poem in a coded communication, the title might be 'My Last Wife' instead of 'My Last Duchess,' by the poet 'Obert Browning' instead of Robert Browning."

"What purpose would that serve?" Violet said.

"The volunteer reading it would notice the mistake," Klaus said. "The changing of certain words or letters is a kind of fluctuation. If you fixed the fluctuations in the poem, you'd receive the message."

"Duchess R?" Fiona asked. "What kind of message is that?"

"I'm not sure," Klaus admitted. "The next page in the book is missing."

"Do you think the missing page is a code, too?" Violet asked.

Klaus shrugged. "I don't know," he said. "Codes are nothing more than a way of talking so that some people understand and other people don't. Remember when we talked to Quigley in the cave, with all the other Snow Scouts listening?"

"Yes," Violet said. "We used words that began with V, F, and D, so that we knew we were all on the same side."

"Maybe we should have a code ourselves," Fiona said, "so that we can communicate if we run into trouble."

"That's a good idea," Klaus said. "What should we use as code words?"

"Food," Sunny suggested.

"Perfect," Violet said. "We'll draw up a list of foods and what they mean in our code. We'll bring them up in conversation, and our enemies will never suspect that we're actually communicating."

"And our enemies could be around any corner," Fiona said, handing the fishbowl of lo mein to Violet and picking up the envelope she had found. "Inside this envelope was a letter. Normally I don't like to read other people's mail, but it seems unlikely that this letter will ever reach Gregor Anwhistle."

"Gregor Anwhistle?" Violet asked. "He's the man who founded the research center. Who was writing to him?"

"A woman named Kit," Fiona said. "I think

it's Kit Snicket—Jacques's sister."

"Of course," Klaus said. "Your stepfather said she was a noble woman who helped build the *Queequeg*."

"According to her letter," Fiona said, "Gregor Anwhistle was involved in something called a 'schism.' What's that?"

"It was a big conflict within V.F.D.," Klaus said. "Quigley told us a little bit about it."

"Everybody chose sides," Violet recalled, "and now the organization is in chaos. Which side was Gregor on?"

"I don't know," Fiona said, frowning. "Some of this letter is in code, and some of it was in water. I can't understand all of it, but it sounds like Gregor was involved with something called Volatile Fungus Deportation."

"'Volatile' means 'unstable,' or 'likely to cause trouble,'" Klaus said. "'Fungus,' of course, means 'mushrooms,' and 'deportation' means 'moving something from one place to another.' Who was moving unstable mushrooms?"

"V.F.D.," Fiona replied. "During the schism, Gregor thought the Medusoid Mycelium might be useful."

"The Medusoid Mycelium?" Violet said, looking nervously at the silent, gray mushrooms that still lined the entrance to the small, tiled room, their black splotches looking particularly eerie in the dim light. "I can't imagine thinking that such deadly things could be useful."

"Listen to what Kit wrote about it," Fiona said. "'The poisonous fungus you insist on cultivating in the grotto will bring grim consequences for all of us. Our factory at Lousy Lane can provide some dilution of the mycelium's destructive respiratory capabilities, and you assure me that the mycelium grows best in small, enclosed spaces, but this is of little comfort. One mistake, Gregor, and your entire facility would have to be abandoned. Please, do not become the thing you dread most by adopting the destructive tactic of our most villainous enemies: playing with fire.'"

Klaus was busily copying Kit Snicket's letter into his commonplace book. "Gregor was growing those mushrooms," he said, "to use on enemies of V.F.D."

"He was going to poison people?" Violet asked.

"Villainous people," Fiona replied, "but Kit Snicket thought that using poisonous mushrooms was equally villainous. They were working on a way to weaken the poison, in a factory on Lousy Lane. But the writer of this letter still thought that Volatile Fungus Deportation was too dangerous, and she warned Gregor that if he wasn't careful, the mycelium would poison the entire research center."

"And now the center is gone," Violet said, "and the mycelium remains. Something went very wrong, right here where we're sitting."

"I still don't understand it," Klaus said. "Was Gregor a villain?"

"I think he was volatile," Fiona said, "like the Medusoid Mycelium. And the writer of this letter says that if you cultivate something volatile, then you're playing with fire."

Violet shuddered, stopped eating her pesto lo mein, and put down the fishbowl. "Playing with fire," of course, is an expression that refers to any dangerous or risky activity, such as writing a letter to a volatile person, or journeying through a dark cave filled with a poisonous fungus in order to search for an object that was taken away quite some time before, and the Baudelaires did not like to think about the fire they were playing with, or the fires that had already been played with in this damp and mysterious room. For a moment, nobody spoke, and the Baudelaires gazed at the stalks and caps of the deadly mushrooms, wondering what had gone wrong with Anwhistle Aquatics. They wondered how the schism began. And they wondered about all of the mysterious and villainous things that seemed to surround the three orphans, drawing closer and closer as their woeful lives went on and on, and if such mysteries would ever be solved and if such villains ever defeated.

"Wane," Sunny said suddenly, and the children saw it was true. The crowd of mushrooms seemed to be just a bit smaller, and here and there they saw a stalk and cap disappear back into the sand, as if the poisonous fungus had decided to implement an alternate strategy, a phrase which here means "would terrorize the Baudelaires in another way."

"Sunny's right," Klaus said with relief. "The Medusoid Mycelium is waning. Soon it'll be safe enough to return to the *Queequeg*."

"It must be a fairly short cycle," Fiona said, making a note in her commonplace book. "How long do you think we've been here?"

"All night, at least," Violet said, unfolding the sheet of newspaper Sunny had found. "It's lucky we found all these materials, otherwise we would have been quite bored."

"My brother always had a deck of cards with him," Fiona remembered, "in case he was stuck in a boring situation. He invented this card game called Fernald's Folly, and we used to play it together whenever we had a long wait."

"Fernald?" Violet asked. "Was that your brother's name?"

"Yes," Fiona said. "Why do you ask?"

"I was just curious," she said, hurriedly tucking the newspaper into the pocket of her uniform. There was just enough room to slip it next to the tin of wasabi.

"Aren't you going to tell us what was in the newspaper?" Klaus asked. "I saw the headline said V.F.D."

"I didn't learn anything," Violet said. "The article was too blurred to read."

"Hmmm," Sunny said, and gave her sister a sly look. The youngest Baudelaire had known Violet since she was born, of course, and found it quite easy to tell when she was lying. Violet looked back at Sunny, and then at Klaus, and shook her head, very, very slightly.

"Why don't we get ready to go?" the eldest

Baudelaire suggested. "By the time we pack up these documents and put on our diving helmets, the fungus will have waned completely."

"You're right," Fiona said. "Here, Sunny, I'll help you get into your helmet. It's the least I can do after you cooked such a delicious meal."

"Shivalrush," Sunny said, which meant "That's very kind of you," and although Fiona had not known Sunny very long, she understood what the youngest Baudelaire had said, more or less, and smiled at all three of the Baudelaire siblings. As the four volunteers suited up—a phrase which here means "prepared their helmets for an underwater journey"—the Baudelaire children felt as if Fiona fit them like a glove—as a friend, or possibly something more. It felt as if Fiona and the Baudelaires were part of the same team, or the same organization, trying to solve the same mysteries and defeat the same villains. It felt that way to the two younger Baudelaires, anyway. Only Violet felt as if their friendship were more volatile, as if Fiona fit her like the wrong glove, or as if their friendship had a tiny flaw—a flaw that might turn into a schism. As Violet put the diving helmet over her head, and made sure that the zipper of the uniform was zipped tight over the portrait of Herman Melville, she heard the slight rustle of the newspaper clipping in her pocket and frowned. She kept frowning as the last of the mushrooms disappeared into the sand, and the four children stepped carefully back into the icy dark water. Because they were traveling against the tide, the volunteers had decided to hold hands, so they would not lose track of one another as they returned to the *Queequeg*, and as their dark journey began, Violet thought of the dangerous and risky secret concealed in her pocket and realized, as Klaus led the way back to the submarine, with Fiona holding Klaus's hand, and Violet holding Fiona's, and Sunny, curled in her helmet, tucked tightly under Violet's arm, that even while swimming in the icy depths of the ocean, the Baudelaires were playing with fire.

The sinister information in the newspaper clipping was like a tiny spore, blossoming in the small, enclosed space of Violet's pocket—like a spore of the deadly Medusoid Mycelium, which at that very moment was blossoming in the small, enclosed space of a diving helmet worn by one of the Baudelaire orphans.

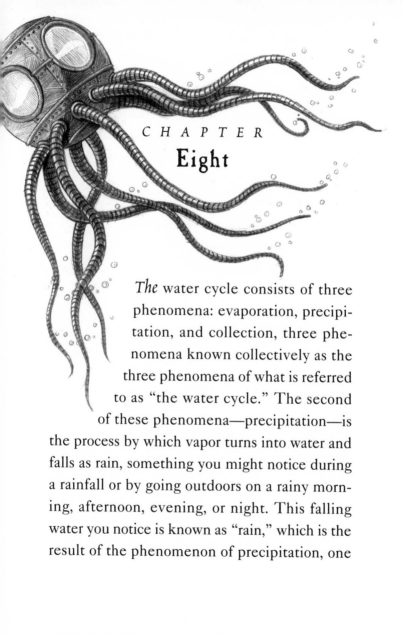

The water cycle consists of three phenomena: evaporation, precipitation, and collection, three phenomena known collectively as the three phenomena of what is referred to as "the water cycle." The second of these phenomena—precipitation—is the process by which vapor turns into water and falls as rain, something you might notice during a rainfall or by going outdoors on a rainy morning, afternoon, evening, or night. This falling water you notice is known as "rain," which is the result of the phenomenon of precipitation, one of the three phenomena that comprise the water cycle. Of these three phenomena, precipitation is regarded as the second one, particularly if a list of the three phenomena places precipitation in the middle, or second, spot on the list. "Precipitation" is quite simply a term for the transformation of vapor into water, which then falls as rain—something you might encounter if you were to step outside during a rainstorm. Rain consists of water, which was formerly vapor but underwent the process known as "precipitation," one of the three phenomena in the water cycle, and by now this tedious description must have put you back to sleep, so you may avoid the gruesome details of my account of Violet, Klaus, and Sunny Baudelaire as they made their way through the Gorgonian Grotto back to the *Queequeg.*

The Baudelaire orphans knew that something was wrong the moment they arrived at the submarine, knocked on the metal hatch, and heard no answer from the captain inside. It had been a dark and cold journey back through the cave, made all the more difficult by the fact that they were swimming against the tide, rather than letting the current carry them along. Klaus, who was leading the way, swept one arm in front of him from side to side, fearful that he would miss the *Queequeg* altogether, or brush his hand against something sinister lurking in the cavern. Fiona trembled throughout the entire journey, and Violet could feel her nervous fingers twitching as she held her hand. And Sunny tried not to panic inside her diving helmet, as her siblings' swim made her bounce up and down in the blackness. The youngest Baudelaire could not see a single light through the small round window in her helmet, but as with all of the Baudelaires, she concentrated on arriving safely, and the thought of returning to the *Queequeg* felt like a small light glowing in the gloom of the grotto. Soon, the Baudelaires thought, they would hear the booming "Aye!" of Captain Widdershins as he welcomed them back from their mission. Perhaps Phil would have cooked them a nice hot meal, even without the culinary assistance of Sunny. And perhaps the telegram device would have received another Volunteer Factual Dispatch, one that might help them find the sugar bowl so their entire journey would not have been a fool's errand. But when Klaus led them to the hatch, they found no sign that anyone aboard the *Queequeg* was welcoming them.

After knocking for several minutes, the worried children had to open the hatch by themselves, a difficult task in the dark, and enter the passageway, quickly closing the hatch behind them. They grew more worried as they discovered that nobody had activated the hatch, so quite a bit of water flowed into the passageway and poured down to the room in which the Baudelaires had first met Captain Widdershins. They could hear the water splashing on the submarine floor as they began their climb down, and strained to hear the captain shouting "Aye!

What a mess!" or "Aye! The valve is broken!" or even something optimistic from Phil, like "Look on the bright side—it's like having a wading pool!"

"Captain Widdershins?" Violet called, her voice muffled through her helmet.

"Stepfather?" Fiona called, her voice muffled through hers.

"Phil?" Klaus called.

"Crew?" Sunny called.

Nobody answered these calls, and nobody commented on the water from the passageway, and when the volunteers reached the end of the passageway and lowered themselves into the small, dim room, they found nobody there to meet them.

"Stepfather?" Fiona called again, but they heard only the movement of the water as it settled into a large puddle on the floor. Without bothering to take off their helmets, the four children splashed through the water and hurried down the hallway, past the plaque with the captain's personal philosophy engraved on it, until they reached the Main Hall. The room was just as enormous as ever, of course, with all of the bewildering pipes, panels, and warning signs, although it seemed as if the place had been tidied up a bit, and there was now a tiny bit of decoration near the wooden table where the Baudelaires had eaten Sunny's chowder and planned their journey through the Gorgonian Grotto. Tied to three chairs were small blue balloons that hovered in the air, and each balloon had a letter printed on its surface in thick, black ink. The first balloon read "V," the second read "F," and only someone as dim as an underwater cave would be surprised to hear that the third read "D."

"V.F.D.," Violet said. "Do you think it's a code?"

"I'm not interested in codes at the moment," Fiona said, her voice tense and echoey inside her helmet. "I want to find my crewmates. Look around, everyone."

The Baudelaires looked around the room,

but it seemed as empty and lonely as the grotto. Without the enormous presence of Captain Widdershins—"enormous presence" is a phrase which here means "large physical size, combined with a vibrant personality and loud voice"—the Main Hall seemed utterly deserted.

"Maybe they're in the kitchen," Klaus said, although it sounded like he didn't believe it himself, "or napping in the barracks."

"They wouldn't have napped," Violet said. "They said they'd be watching us the entire time."

Fiona took a step toward the door to the kitchen, but then stopped and looked at the wooden table. "Their helmets are gone," she said. "Both Phil and my stepfather were keeping their diving helmets on the table, in case of an emergency." She ran her hand along the table, as if she could make the helmets reappear. "They're gone," she said. "They've left the *Queequeg.*"

"I can't believe that," Klaus said, shaking his

head. "They knew we were traveling through the grotto. They wouldn't abandon their fellow volunteers."

"Maybe they thought we weren't coming back," Fiona said.

"No," Violet said, pointing to a panel on the wall. "They could see us. We were tiny green dots on the sonar detector."

The children looked at the sonar panel, hoping to see dots that might represent their missing crewmates. "They must have had a very good reason to leave," Fiona said.

"What reason could there be?" Klaus said. "No matter what occurred, they would have waited for us."

"No," Fiona said. Sadly, she removed her diving helmet, and the middle Baudelaire saw she had tears in her eyes. "No matter what occurred," she said, "my stepfather wouldn't have hesitated. He or she who hesitates is . . ."

"Lost," Klaus finished for her, and put his hand on her shoulder.

"Maybe they didn't go of their own volition," Violet said, using a phrase which here means "by choice." "Maybe somebody took them."

"Took the crew away," Klaus said, "and left behind three balloons?"

"It's a mystery," Violet said, "but I'm sure it's one we can solve. Let's just take off our helmets, and we can get to work."

Klaus nodded, and removed his diving helmet, putting it down on the floor next to Fiona's. Violet removed hers, and then went to open the tiny door of Sunny's helmet, so the youngest Baudelaire could uncurl herself from the small, enclosed space and join her siblings. But Fiona grabbed Violet's hand before it reached the helmet, and stopped her, pointing through the small round window in Sunny's helmet.

There are many things in this world that are difficult to see. An ice cube in a glass of water, for instance, might pass unnoticed, particularly if the ice cube is small, and the glass of water is ten miles in diameter. A short woman might be difficult to see on a crowded city street, particularly if she has disguised herself as a mailbox, and people keep putting letters in her mouth. And a small, ceramic bowl, with a tight-fitting lid to keep something important inside, might be difficult to find in the laundry room of an enormous hotel, particularly if there were a terrible villain nearby, making you feel nervous and distracted. But there are also things that are difficult to see not because of the size of their surroundings, or a clever disguise, or a treacherous person with a book of matches in his pocket and a fiendish plot in his brain, but because the things are so upsetting to look at, so distressing to believe, that it is as if your eyes refuse to see what is right in front of them. You can glance into a mirror, and not see how old you are growing, or how unattractive your hairstyle has become, until someone kindly points those things out to you. You can gaze upon a place you once lived, and not see how terribly the building has changed, or how sinister the neighborhood has become, until you walk a few paces to an ice-cream store and notice that your favorite flavor has been discontinued. And you can stare into the small, round window of a diving helmet, as Violet and Klaus did at that moment, and not see the stalks and caps of a terrible gray fungus growing poisonously on the glass, until someone utters its scientific name in a horrified whisper. "It's the Medusoid Mycelium," Fiona said, and the two elder Baudelaires blinked and saw that it was so.

"Oh no," Violet murmured. *"Oh no!"*

"Get her out!" Klaus cried. "Get Sunny out at once, or she'll be poisoned!"

"No!" Fiona said, and snatched the helmet away from the siblings. She put it down on the table as if it were a tureen, a word which here means "a wide, deep dish used for serving stew or soup, instead of a small, terrified girl curled up in a piece of deep-sea equipment." "The diving helmet can serve as quarantine. If we open it, the fungus will spread. The entire submarine could become a field of mushrooms."

"We can't leave our sister in there!" Violet cried. "The spores will poison her!"

"She's probably been poisoned already," Fiona said quietly. "In a small, enclosed space like that helmet, there's no way she could escape."

"That can't be true," Klaus said, taking off his glasses as if refusing to see the horror of their situation. But at that moment their predicament became perfectly clear, as the children heard a small, eerie sound come from the helmet. It reminded Violet and Klaus of the fish of the Stricken Stream, struggling to breathe in the ashy, black waters. Sunny was coughing.

"Sunny!" Klaus shouted into the helmet.

"Malady," Sunny said, which meant "I'm beginning to feel unwell."

"Don't talk, Sunny!" Fiona called through the tiny window of the helmet, and turned to the elder Baudelaires. "The mycelium has

destructive respiratory capabilities," the mycologist explained, walking over to the sideboard.
"That's what it said in that letter. Your sister
should save her breath. The spores will make it
more and more difficult for Sunny to talk, and
she'll probably start coughing as the fungus
grows inside her. In an hour's time, she won't
be able to breathe. It would be fascinating if it
weren't so horrible."

"*Fascinating?*" Violet covered her mouth
with her hands and shut her eyes, trying not to
imagine what her terrified sister was feeling.
"What can we do?" she asked.

"We can make an antidote," Fiona said.
"There must be some useful information in my
mycological library."

"I'll help," Klaus said. "I'm sure I'll find the
books difficult to read, but—"

"No," Fiona said. "I need to be alone to do
my research. You and Violet should climb that
rope ladder and fire up the engines so we can
get out of this cave."

"But we should all do the research!" Violet cried. "We only have an hour, or maybe even less! If the mushrooms grew while we swam back to the *Queequeg*, then—"

"Then we certainly don't have time to argue," Fiona finished, opening the cabinet and removing a large pile of books. "I order you to leave me alone, so I can do this research and save your sister!"

The elder Baudelaires looked at one another, and then at the diving helmet on the table. "You *order* us?" Klaus asked.

"Aye!" Fiona cried, and the children realized it was the first time the mycologist had uttered that word. "I'm in charge here! With my stepfather gone, I am the captain of the *Queequeg*! Aye!"

"It doesn't matter who the captain is!" Violet said. "The important thing is to save my sister!"

"Climb up that rope ladder!" Fiona cried.

"Aye! Fire up those engines! Aye! We're going to save Sunny! Aye! And find my stepfather! Aye! And retrieve the sugar bowl! Aye! And it's no time to hesitate! She who hesitates is lost! That's my personal philosophy!"

"That's the captain's personal philosophy," Klaus said, "not yours."

"I am the captain!" Fiona said fiercely. The middle Baudelaire could see that behind her triangular glasses, the mycologist was crying. "Go and do what I say."

Klaus opened his mouth to say something more, but found that he, too, was crying, and without another word turned from his friend and walked over to the rope ladder, with Violet following behind.

"*She's wrong!*" the eldest Baudelaire whispered furiously. "You know she's wrong, Klaus. What are we going to do?"

"We're going to fire up the engines," Klaus said, "and steer the *Queequeg* out of this cave."

"But that won't save Sunny," Violet said. "Don't you remember the description of the Medusoid Mycelium?"

"'*A single spore has such grim power,*'" Klaus recited, "'*That you may die within the hour.*' Of course I remember."

"Hour?" Sunny said fearfully from inside her helmet.

"Shush," Violet said. "Save your breath, Sunny. We'll find a way to cure you right away."

"Not right away," Klaus corrected sadly. "Fiona is the captain now, and she ordered us—"

"I don't care about Fiona's orders," Violet said. "She's too volatile to get us out of this situation—just like her stepfather, and just like her brother!" The eldest Baudelaire reached into the pocket of her uniform and drew out the newspaper clipping she had taken from the grotto. Her hand brushed against the tin of wasabi, and she shivered, hoping that her sister would recuperate and live to use the Japanese condiment in one of her recipes. "Listen to this, Klaus!"

"I don't want to listen!" Klaus said in an angry whisper. "Maybe Fiona is right! Maybe we shouldn't hesitate, particularly at a time like this! If we don't get an antidote to our sister, she might perish! Hesitating will only make things worse!"

"Firing up the engines, instead of helping Fiona with her research, will only make things worse!" Violet said.

At that moment, however, both Violet and Klaus saw something that made things worse, and they realized that they both had been wrong. The two Baudelaires shouldn't have been firing up the engines of the *Queequeg*, and they shouldn't have been helping Fiona with her research, and they shouldn't have been arguing with one another. The Baudelaires, and Fiona, too, should have been standing very still, trying not to make even the smallest noise, and instead of looking at the diving helmet, where their sister was suffering under the poison of the Medusoid Mycelium, they should have been looking at the submarine's sonar detector, or out of the porthole over the table, which looked out into the dark depths of the cave. On the green panel was the glowing Q, representing the *Queequeg*, but this was another thing in the world that was difficult to see, because another glowing green symbol was occupying the very same space. And outside the porthole was a mass of small, metal tubes, circling in the gloomy water and making thousands and thousands of bubbles, and in the middle of all those tubes was a large, open space, like a gigantic hungry mouth—the mouth of an octopus, about to devour the *Queequeg* and all its remaining crew. The image on the sonar detector, of course, was an eye, and the view from the porthole was of a submarine, but either way the children knew it was Count Olaf, and that made things much, much worse indeed.

CHAPTER Nine

If you are considering a life of villainy—and I certainly hope that you are not—there are a few things that appear to be necessary to every villain's success. One thing is a villainous disregard for other people, so that a villain may talk to his or her victims impolitely, ignore their pleas for mercy, and even behave violently toward them if the villain is in the mood for that sort

of thing. Another thing villains require is a villainous imagination, so that they might spend their free time dreaming up treacherous schemes in order to further their villainous careers. Villains require a small group of villainous cohorts, who can be persuaded to serve the villain in a henchpersonal capacity. And villains need to develop a villainous laugh, so that they may simultaneously celebrate their villainous deeds and frighten whatever nonvillainous people happen to be nearby. A successful villain should have all of these things at his or her villainous fingertips, or else give up villainy altogether and try to lead a life of decency, integrity, and kindness, which is much more challenging and noble, if not always quite as exciting.

Count Olaf, of course, was an excellent villain, a phrase which here means "someone particularly skilled at villainy" rather than "a villain with several desirable qualities," and the Baudelaire orphans had known this soon after that terrible day at Briny Beach, when the

children learned of the terrible fire that began
so many of the unfortunate events in their lives.
But as the *Queequeg* tumbled into the mouth of
his dreadful octopus submarine, it seemed to
the orphans that the villain had become even
more villainous during his brief absence from
their lives. Olaf had proven his villainous disregard for other people over and over, from his
vicious murder of the children's guardians to his
affinity for arson, a phrase which here means
"enthusiasm for burning down buildings, no
matter how many people were inside," but the
children realized that Olaf's disregard had
become even more dreadful, as the *Queequeg*
passed through the gaping mouth and was
roughly tossed from side to side in a mechanical imitation of swallowing, forcing Violet and
Klaus—and Fiona, too, of course—to hang on
for dear life as the Main Hall rolled this way and
that, spinning Sunny in her helmet like a water-
melon in a washing machine. The count had dis-
played his villainous imagination on a number

of occasions, from his dastardly schemes to steal the Baudelaire fortune to his nefarious plots to kidnap Duncan and Isadora Quagmire, but the siblings gazed out of the porthole and saw that Olaf's infernal imagination had run utterly wild in decorating this terrible submarine, for the *Queequeg* rolled along a rumbling tunnel that was almost as dark and threatening as the Gorgonian Grotto, with every inch of its metallic walls covered in eerie glowing eyes. The count always had an assortment of cohorts, from his original theatrical troupe—many of whom were no longer with him—to some former employees of Caligari Carnival, but the orphans saw that he had lured many others to join him when the tunnel rounded a corner and the elder Baudelaires had a brief glimpse of an enormous room full of people rowing long, metal oars, activating the terrible metal arms of the octopus. And, perhaps worst of all, when the *Queequeg* finally came to a shuddering stop and Violet and Klaus looked out of the porthole, they learned that the villain had clearly been rehearsing his villainous laugh until it was extra wicked and more theatrical than ever. Count Olaf was standing on a small, metal platform with a triumphant grin on his face, dressed in a familiar suit made of slippery-looking material, but with a portrait of another author whom only a very devoted reader would recognize, and when he peered through the porthole and spied the frightened children, he opened his mouth and began his new villainous laugh, which included new wheezes, bonus snarls, and an assortment of strange syllables the Baudelaires had never heard.

"Ha ha ha heepa-heepa ho!" he cried. "Tee hee tort tort tort! Hot cha ha ha! Sniggle hee! Ha, if I do say so myself!" With a boastful gesture, he hopped off the platform, drew a long, sharp sword, and quickly traced a circle on the glass of the porthole. Violet and Klaus covered their ears as the sword shrieked its way around the window. Then, with one flick of his sword,

Olaf sent the glass circle tumbling into the Main Hall, where it lay unbroken on the floor, and leaped through the porthole onto the large, wooden table to laugh at them further. "I'm splitting my sides!" he cried. "I'm rolling in the aisles! I'm nauseous with mirth! I'm rattling with glee! I'm seriously considering compiling a joke book from all of the hilarious things bouncing around my brain! Hup hup ha ha hammy hee hee!"

Violet dashed forward and grabbed the helmet in which Sunny was still curled, so Olaf would not kick it as he pranced triumphantly on top of the table. She could not bear to think of her sister, who was inhaling the poison of the Medusoid Mycelium as Olaf wasted precious minutes performing his tiresome new laugh. "Stop laughing, Count Olaf," she said. "There's nothing funny about villainy."

"Sure there is!" Olaf crowed. "Ha ha hat rack! Just think of it! I made my way down the mountain and found pieces of your toboggan scattered all over some very sharp rocks! Tee hee torpid sniggle! I thought you had drowned in the Stricken Stream and were swimming with all those coughing fishes! Ho ho hagfish! I was brokenhearted!"

"You weren't brokenhearted," Klaus said. "You've tried to destroy us plenty of times."

"That's why I was brokenhearted!" Olaf cried. "Ho ho sniggle! I personally planned to slaughter you Baudelaires myself, after I had your fortune of course, and pry the sugar bowl out of your dead fingers or toes!"

Violet and Klaus looked at one another hurriedly. They had almost forgotten telling Olaf that they knew the location of the sugar bowl, even though they of course had no idea of its whereabouts. "To cheer myself up," the villain continued, "I met my associates at the Hotel Denouement, where they were cooking up a little scheme of their own, and convinced them to lend me a handful of our new recruits." The elder Baudelaires knew that the associates were the man with a beard and no hair, and the woman with hair but no beard, two people so sinister that even Olaf seemed to find them a bit frightening, and that the new recruits were a group of Snow Scouts that these villains had recently kidnapped. "Tee hee turncoat! Thanks to their generosity, I was able to get this submarine working again! Sniggle ha ho ho! Of course, I need to be back at the Hotel Denouement before Thursday, but in the meantime I had a few days to kill, so I thought I'd kill some of my old enemies! Hee hee halbert sniggle! So I began roaming around the sea, looking for Captain Widdershins and his idiotic submarine on my sonar detector! Tee hee telotaxis! But now that I've captured the *Queequeg*, I find you Baudelaires aboard! It's hilarious! It's humorous! It's droll! It's relatively amusing!"

"How dare you capture this submarine!" Fiona cried. "I'm the captain of the *Queequeg*, and I demand that you return us to the sea at once! Aye!"

Count Olaf peered down at the mycologist. "*Aye?*" he repeated. "You must be Fiona, that little fungus freak! Why, you're all grown up! The last time I saw you I was trying to throw thumbtacks into your cradle! Ha ha hoi polloi! What happened to Widdershins? Why isn't he the captain?"

"My stepfather is not around at the moment," Fiona replied, blinking behind her triangular glasses.

"Tee hee terry cloth!" Count Olaf said. "Your stepfather has abandoned you, eh? Well, I suppose it was only a matter of time. Your whole family could never choose which side of the schism was theirs. Your brother used to be a goody-goody as well, trying to prevent fires instead of encouraging them, but eventually—"

"My stepfather has not abandoned me," Fiona said, though her voice faltered a bit, a phrase which here means "sounded as if she weren't so sure." She did not even add an "Aye!" to her sentence.

"We'll see about that," Olaf said, grinning wickedly. "I'm going to lock all of you in the brig, which is the official seafaring term for 'jail.'"

"We know what the brig is," Klaus said.

"Then you know it's not a very pleasant place," the villain said. "The previous owner used it to hold traitors captive, and I see no reason to break with tradition."

"We're not traitors, and we're not leaving the *Queequeg*," Violet said, and held up the diving helmet. Sunny tried to say something, but the growing fungus made her cough instead, and Olaf frowned at the coughing helmet.

"What's that?" he demanded

"Sunny is in here," she said. "And she's very ill."

"I was wondering where the baby brat was," Count Olaf said. "I was hoping she was trapped underneath my shoe, but I see that it's just some ridiculous book." He lifted his slippery foot to reveal *Mushroom Minutiae*, the book Fiona had been using for her research, and kicked it off the table where it skittered into a far corner.

"There is a very deadly poison inside that helmet," Fiona said, staring at the book in frustration. "Aye! If Sunny doesn't receive an antidote within the hour, she will perish."

"What do I care?" Olaf growled, once again showing his villainous disregard for other people. "I only need one Baudelaire to get my hands on the fortune. Now come with me! Ha ha handiwork!"

"We're staying right here," Klaus said. "Our sister's life depends on it."

Count Olaf drew his sword again, and traced a sinister shape in the air. "I'll tell you what your lives depend on," he said. "Your lives depend on me! If I wanted, I could drown you in the sea, or have you strangled by the arms of the mechanical octopus! It's only out of the kindness of my heart, and because of my own greed, that I'm locking you in the brig instead!"

Sunny coughed inside her helmet, and Violet thought quickly. "If you let us help our sister," she said, "we'll tell you where the sugar bowl is."

Count Olaf's eyes narrowed, and he gave the children a wide, toothy grin the two Baudelaires remembered from so many of their troubled times. His eyes shone brightly, as if he were telling a joke as nasty as his unbrushed teeth. "You can't try that trick again," he sneered. "I'm not going to bargain with an orphan, no matter how pretty she may be. Once you get to the brig, you'll reveal where the sugar bowl is— once my henchman gets his hands on you. Or should I say *hooks*? Tee hee torture!"

Count Olaf leaped back through the porthole as Violet and Klaus looked at one another in fear. They knew Count Olaf was referring to the hook-handed man, who had been working with the villain as long as they had known him and was one of their least favorite of Olaf's comrades. "I could race up the rope ladder," Violet murmured to the others, "and fire up the engines of the *Queequeg*."

"We can't take the submarine underwater with the window gone," Fiona said. "We'd drown."

Klaus put his ear to the diving helmet, and heard his sister whimper, and then cough. "But how can we save Sunny?" he asked. "Time is running out."

Fiona eyed the far corner of the room. "I'll take that book with me," she said, "and—"

"*Hurry up!*" Count Olaf cried. "I can't stand around all day! I have plenty of people to boss around!"

"Aye!" Fiona said, as Violet, still holding Sunny, led Klaus through the porthole to join Count Olaf on the platform. "I'll be there in a second," she said, and the mycologist took one hesitant step toward *Mushroom Minutiae*.

"You'll be there *now*!" Olaf growled, and shook his sword at her. "He who hesitates is lost! Hee hee sniggle!"

At the mention of the captain's personal

philosophy, Fiona sighed, and stopped her furtive journey—a phrase which here means "sneaking"—toward the mycological book. "Or she," she said quietly, and stepped through the porthole to join the Baudelaires.

"On the way to the brig, I'll give you the grand tour!" Olaf announced, leading the way out of the round, metal room that was serving as a sort of brig for the *Queequeg* itself. There were several inches of water on the floor, to help the captured submarine move through the tunnel, and the Baudelaires' boots made loud, wet splashes as they followed the boasting villain. While Sunny coughed again in her helmet, Olaf pressed an eye on the wall, and a small door slid open with a sinister whisper to reveal a corridor. "This submarine is one of the greatest things I've ever stolen," he bragged. "It has everything I'll need to defeat V.F.D. once and for all. It has a sonar system, so I can rid the seas of V.F.D. submarines. It has an enormous flyswatter, so I can rid the skies of V.F.D.

planes. It has a lifetime supply of matches, so I can rid the world of V.F.D. headquarters. It has several cases of wine that I plan to drink up myself, and a closet full of very stylish outfits for my girlfriend. And best of all, it has plenty of opportunities for children to do hard labor! Ha ha hedonism!"

Gesturing with his sword, he led the children around a corner into an enormous room—the room they'd had a glimpse of as the *Queequeg* tumbled inside this terrible place. It was quite dark, with only a few lanterns hanging from the tops of tall pillars scattered around the room, but Violet and Klaus could see two large rows of uncomfortable-looking wooden benches, on which sat a crowd of children, hurriedly working long oars that stretched across the room and even beyond the walls, where they slid through metal holes in order to control the tentacles of the octopus. The elder Baudelaires recognized some of the children from a troop of Snow Scouts they had encountered in the Mortmain

Mountains, and a few looked quite a bit like other students at Prufrock Preparatory School, where the siblings had first encountered Carmelita Spats, but some of the others were children with whom the Baudelaires had had no prior experience, a phrase which here means "who had probably been kidnapped by Count Olaf or his associates on another occasion." The children looked very weary, quite hungry, and more than a little bored as they worked the metal oars back and forth. In the very center of the room appeared to be another octopus—this one made of slippery cloth. Six of the octopus's arms hung limply at its sides, but two of them were waving high in the air, one of them clutching what looked like a long, damp noodle.

"Row faster, you stupid brats!" the octopus cried in a familiar, wicked voice. "We have to get back to the Hotel Denouement before Thursday, and it's Monday already! If you don't hurry up I'm going to hit you with this tagliatelle grande! I warn you, being struck with a large piece of pasta is an unpleasant and some-what sticky experience! Ho ho sniggle!"

"Hee hee snaggle!" Olaf cried in agreement, and the octopus whirled around.

"Darling!" it cried, and the siblings were not surprised to see that it was Esmé Squalor, Count Olaf's treacherous girlfriend, in another one of her absurd, stylish outfits. Using the slippery cloth of the submarine's uniforms, the villain-ous girlfriend had fashioned an octopus dress, with two large plastic eyes, six extra sleeves, and suction cups stuck all over her boots, just as real octopi have on their tentacles to help them move around. Esmé took a few sticky steps toward Olaf and then peered at the children beneath the slippery hood of the dress. "Are these the *Baudelaires*?" she asked in astonish-ment. "How can that be? We already celebrated their deaths!"

"It turns out they survived," Count Olaf said, "but their good luck is about to come to an end. I'm taking them to the brig!"

"The baby certainly has grown," Esmé said, peering at Fiona. "But she's just as ugly as she ever was."

"No, no," Olaf said. "The baby's locked up in that helmet, coughing her little lungs out. This is Fiona, Captain Widdershin's stepdaughter. The captain abandoned her!"

"Abandoned her?" Esmé repeated. "How in! How stylish! How marvelous! This calls for more of our new laughter! Ha ha hedgehog!"

"Tee hee tempeh!" Olaf cackled. "Life keeps getting better and better!"

"Sniggle ho ho!" Esmé shrieked. "Our triumph is just around the corner!"

"Ha ha Hepplewhite!" Olaf crowed. "V.F.D. will be reduced to ashes forever!"

"Giggle giggle glandular problems!" Esmé cried. "We are going to be painfully wealthy!"

"Heepa deepa ho ho ha!" Olaf shouted. "The world will always remember the name of this wonderful submarine!"

"What is the name of this submarine?" Fiona

asked, and to the children's relief the villains stopped their irritating laughter. Olaf glared at the mycologist and then looked at the ground.

"The *Carmelita*," he admitted quietly. "I wanted to call it the *Olaf*, but somebody made me change it."

"The *Olaf* is a cakesniffing name!" cried a rude voice the siblings had hoped never to hear again, and I'm sorry to say that Carmelita Spats skipped into the room, sneering at the Baudelaires as she did so. Carmelita had always been the sort of unpleasant person who believed that she was prettier and smarter than everybody else, and Violet and Klaus saw instantly that she had become even more spoiled under the care of Olaf and Esmé. She was dressed in an outfit perhaps even more absurd than Esmé Squalor's, in different shades of pink so blinding that Violet and Klaus had to squint in order to look at her. Around her waist was a wide, frilly tutu, which is a skirt used during ballet performances, and on her head was an enormous pink crown decorated with light pink ribbons and dark pink flowers. She had two pink wings taped to her back, two pink hearts drawn on her cheeks, and two different pink shoes on each foot that made unpleasant slapping sounds as she walked. Around her neck was a stethoscope, such as doctors use, with pink puffballs pasted all over it, and in one hand she had a long pink wand with a bright pink star at the end of it.

"Stop looking at my outfit!" she commanded the Baudelaires scornfully. "You're just jealous of me because I'm a tap-dancing ballerina fairy princess veterinarian!"

"You look adorable, darling," purred Esmé, patting her on the crown. "Doesn't she look adorable, Olaf?"

"I suppose so," Count Olaf muttered. "I wish you would ask me before taking disguises from my trunk."

"But Countie, I needed your disguises," Carmelita whined, batting her eyelashes, which were covered in pink glitter. "I needed a special outfit for my special tap-dancing ballerina fairy princess veterinarian dance recital!"

Several of the children groaned at their oars. "Please, no!" cried one of the Snow Scouts. "Her dance recitals last for hours!"

"Have mercy on us!" cried another child.

"Carmelita Spats is the most talented dancer in the entire universe!" Esmé growled, snapping the noodle over the rower's heads. "You brats should be grateful that she is performing for you! It'll help you row!"

"Ugh," Sunny could not help saying from inside her helmet, as if the idea of Carmelita's dance recital were making her even sicker. The elder Baudelaires looked at one another and tried to imagine how they could help their young sibling. "I think we have a pink cape aboard the *Queequeg*," Klaus said hurriedly. "It would look perfect on Carmelita. I'll just run back to the submarine, and—"

"I don't want your old clothes, you cakesniffer!" Carmelita said scornfully. "A tap-dancing ballerina fairy princess veterinarian doesn't wear hand-me-downs!"

"Isn't she precious?" Esmé cooed. "She's like the adopted child I never had—except for you Baudelaires, of course. But I never liked you much."

"Are you going to stay and watch me, Countie?" Carmelita asked. "This is going to be the most special dance recital in the whole wide world!"

"There's too much work to do," Count Olaf said hastily. "I have to throw these children in the brig, so my associate can force them to reveal the location of the sugar bowl."

"You like that sugar bowl more than me," Carmelita pouted.

"Of course we don't, darling," Esmé said. "Olaf, tell her that sugar bowl doesn't mean a thing to you! Tell her she's like a wonderful marshmallow in the middle of our lives!"

"You're a marshmallow, Carmelita," Olaf

said, and pushed the children out of the enormous room. "I'll see you later."

"Tell Hooky to be extra vicious with those brats!" Esmé cried, whipping the tagliatelle grande over her fake octopus head. "And now, on with the show!"

Count Olaf ushered the children out of the room as Carmelita Spats began tapping and twirling in front of the rowers. The elder Baudelaires were almost grateful to go to the brig, rather than being forced to watch a tap-dancing ballerina fairy princess veterinarian dance recital. Olaf dragged them down another hallway that twisted every which way, curving to the right and to the left as if it were a snake the mechanical octopus had eaten, and finally stopped in front of a small door, with a metal eye where the doorknob ought to have been.

"This is the brig!" Count Olaf cried. "Ha ha haberdashery!"

Sunny coughed once more from inside her

helmet—a rough, loud cough that sounded worse than before. The Medusoid Mycelium was clearly continuing its ghastly growth, and Violet tried one more time to convince the villain to let them help her. "Please let us go back to the *Queequeg*," she said. "Can't you hear her coughing?"

"Yes," Count Olaf said, "but I don't care."

"*Please!*" Klaus cried. "This is a matter of life and death!"

"It certainly is," Olaf sneered, turning the knob. "My associate will make you reveal the location of the sugar bowl if he has to tear you apart to do it!"

"Listen to my friends!" Fiona said. "Aye! We're in a terrible situation!"

"Oh, I wouldn't say that," Count Olaf said, with a wicked smile, as the door creaked open to reveal a small, bare room. There was nothing in it but a small stool, at which a man sat, shuffling a deck of cards with quite a bit of difficulty. "How can a family reunion be a terrible situation?" Olaf said, and shoved the children inside the room, slamming the door behind them.

Violet and Klaus faced Olaf's associate, and turned the diving helmet so Sunny could face him, too. The siblings were not surprised, of course, that the person shuffling the cards was the hook-handed man, and they were not at all happy to see him, and they were quite scared that their time in the brig would make it impossible to save Sunny from the mushrooms growing inside her helmet. But when they looked at Fiona, they saw that the mycologist was quite surprised at who she saw in the brig, and quite happy to see the man who stood up from his stool and waved his hooks in amazement.

"Fiona!" the hook-handed man cried.

"Fernald!" Fiona said, and it seemed they just might save Sunny after all.

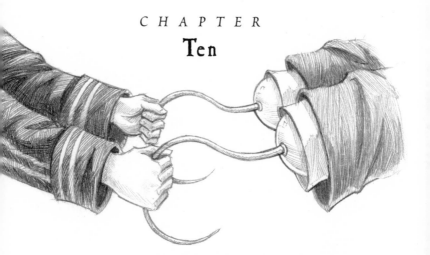

The way sadness works is one of the strange riddles of the world. If you are stricken with a great sadness, you may feel as if you have been set aflame, not only because of the enormous pain, but also because your sadness may spread over your life, like smoke from an enormous fire. You might find it difficult to see anything but your own sadness, the way smoke can cover a landscape so that all anyone can see is black. You may find that happy things are tainted with sadness, the way smoke leaves its ashen colors and scents on everything it touches. And you may find that if someone pours water all over you, you are damp and distracted, but not cured of your sadness, the way a fire department can douse a fire but never recover what has been burnt down. The Baudelaire orphans, of course, had had a great sadness in their life from the moment they first heard of their parents' death, and sometimes it felt as if they had to wave smoke away from their eyes to see even the happiest of moments. As Violet and Klaus watched Fiona and the hook-handed man embrace one another, they felt as if the smoke of their own unhappiness had filled the brig. They could not bear to think that Fiona had found her long-lost brother when they them-selves, in all likelihood, would never see their parents again, and might even lose their sister as the poisonous spores of the Medusoid Mycelium made her coughing sound worse and worse inside the helmet.

"Fiona!" the hook-handed man cried. "Is it really you?"

"Aye," the mycologist said, taking off her triangular glasses to wipe away her tears. "I never thought I would see you again, Fernald. What happened to your hands?"

"Never mind that," the hook-handed man said quickly. "Why are you here? Did you join Count Olaf, too?"

"Certainly not," Fiona said firmly. "He captured the *Queequeg*, and threw us into the brig."

"So you've joined the Baudelaire brats," the hook-handed man said. "I should have known you were a goody-goody!"

"I haven't joined the Baudelaires," Fiona said, just as firmly. "They've joined me. Aye! I'm the captain of the *Queequeg* now."

"You?" said Olaf's henchman. "What happened to Widdershins?"

"He disappeared from the submarine," Fiona replied. "We don't know where he is."

"I don't care where he is," the hook-handed

man sneered. "I couldn't care less about that mustached fool! He's the reason I joined Count Olaf in the first place! The captain was always shouting 'Aye! Aye! Aye!' and ordering me around! So I ran away and joined Olaf's acting troupe!"

"But Count Olaf is a terrible villain!" Fiona cried. "He has no regard for other people. He dreams up treacherous schemes, and lures others into becoming his cohorts!"

"Those are just the bad aspects of him," the hook-handed man said. "There are many good parts, as well. For instance, he has a wonderful laugh."

"A wonderful laugh is no excuse for villainous behavior!" Fiona said.

"Let's just agree to disagree," the hook-handed man replied, using a tiresome expression which here means "You're probably right, but I'm too embarrassed to admit it." He waved one hook carelessly at his sister. "Step aside, Fiona. It's time for the orphans to tell me where the sugar bowl is."

Olaf's henchman scraped his hooks together to give them a quick sharpening, and took one threatening step toward the Baudelaires. Violet and Klaus looked at one another in fear, and then at the diving helmet, where they heard their sister give another shuddering cough, and knew that it was time to lay their cards on the table, a phrase which here means "reveal themselves honestly to Olaf's wicked henchman."

"We don't know where the sugar bowl is," Violet said.

"My sister is telling the truth," Klaus said. "Do with us what you will, but we won't be able to tell you anything."

The hook-handed man glared at them, and scraped his hooks together once more. "You're liars," he said. "Both of you are rotten orphan *liars.*"

"It's true, Fernald," Fiona said. "Aye! Finding the sugar bowl was the *Queequeg*'s mission, but so far we've failed."

"If you don't know where the sugar bowl is,"

the hook-handed man said angrily, "then putting you in the brig is completely pointless!" He turned around and kicked his small stool, toppling it over, and then kicked the wall of the brig for good measure. "What am I supposed to do now?" he sulked.

Fiona put her hand on her brother's hook. "Take us back to the *Queequeg*," she said. "Sunny is in that helmet, along with a growth of Medusoid Mycelium."

"Medusoid Mycelium?" Olaf's henchman repeated in horror. "That's a very dangerous fungus!"

"She's in great danger," Violet said. "If we don't find a cure very, very soon, she'll die."

The hook-handed man frowned, but then looked at the helmet and gave the children a shrug. "Why should I care if she dies?" he asked. "She's made my life miserable from the time I met her. Every time we fail to get the Baudelaire fortune, Count Olaf yells at everyone!"

"You're the one who made the Baudelaires' lives miserable," Fiona said. "Count Olaf has performed countless treacherous schemes, and you helped him time and time again. Aye! You ought to be ashamed of yourself."

The hook-handed man sighed, and looked down at the floor of the brig. "Sometimes I am," he admitted. "Life in Olaf's troupe sounded like it was going to be glamorous and fun, but we've ended up doing more murder, arson, blackmail, and assorted violence than I would have preferred."

"This is your chance to do something noble," Fiona said. "You don't have to remain on the wrong side of the schism."

"Oh, Fiona," the hook-handed man said, and put one hook awkwardly around her shoulder. "You don't understand. There is no wrong side of the schism."

"Of course there is," Klaus said. "V.F.D. is a noble organization, and Count Olaf is a terrible villain."

"A noble organization?" the hook-handed man said. "Is that so? Tell that to your baby sister, you four-eyed fool! If it weren't for Volatile Fungus Deportation, you never would have encountered those deadly mushrooms!"

The children looked at one another, remembering what they had read in the Gorgonian Grotto. They had to admit that Olaf's henchman was right. But Violet reached into her pocket and drew out the newspaper clipping Sunny had found in the cave. She held it out so everyone could see the *Daily Punctilio* article that the eldest Baudelaire had kept hidden for so long.

"'VERIFYING FERNALD'S DEFECTION,'" she said, reading the headline out loud, and then continued by reading the byline, a word which here means "name of the person who wrote the article." "'By Jacques Snicket. It has now been confirmed that the fire that destroyed Anwhistle Aquatics, and took the life of famed ichnologist Gregor Anwhistle, was set by Fernald

Widdershins, the son of the captain of the *Queequeg* submarine. The Widdershins family's participation in a recent schism has raised several questions regarding. . .'" Violet looked up and met the glare of Olaf's henchman. "The rest of the article is blurry," she said, "but the truth is clear. You defected—you abandoned V.F.D. and joined up with Olaf!"

"The difference between the two sides of the schism," Klaus said, "is that one side puts out fires, and the other starts them."

The hook-handed man reached forward and speared the article on one of his hooks, and then turned the clipping around so he could read it again. "You should have seen the fire," he said quietly. "From a distance, it looked like an enormous black plume of smoke, rising straight out of the water. It was like the entire sea was burning down."

"You must have been proud of your handiwork," Fiona said bitterly.

"Proud?" the hook-handed man said. "It

was the worst day of my life. That plume of smoke was the saddest thing I ever saw." He speared the newspaper with his other hook and ripped the article into shreds. "The *Punctilio* got everything wrong," he said. "Captain Widdershins isn't my father. Widdershins isn't my last name. And there's much more to the fire than that. You should know that the *Daily Punctilio* doesn't tell the whole story, Baudelaires. Just as the poison of a deadly fungus can be the source of some wonderful medicines, someone like Jacques Snicket can do something villainous, and someone like Count Olaf can do something noble. Even your parents—"

"Our stepfather knew Jacques Snicket," Fiona said. "He was a good man, but Count Olaf murdered him. Are you a murderer, too? Did you kill Gregor Anwhistle?"

In grim silence, the hook-handed man held his hooks in front of the children. "The last time you saw me," he said to Fiona, "I had two hands, instead of hooks. Our stepfather probably didn't tell you what happened to me—he always said there were secrets in this world too terrible for young people to know. What a fool!"

"Our stepfather isn't a fool," Fiona said. "He's a noble man. Aye!"

"People aren't either wicked or noble," the hook-handed man said. "They're like chef's salads, with good things and bad things chopped and mixed together in a vinaigrette of confusion and conflict." He turned to the two elder Baudelaires and pointed at them with his hooks. "Look at yourselves, Baudelaires. Do you really think we're so different? When those eagles carried me away from the mountains in that net, I saw the ruins of that fire in the hinterlands—a fire we started together. You've burned things down, and so have I. You joined the crew of the *Queequeg*, and I joined the crew of the *Carmelita*. Our captains are both volatile people, and we're both trying to get to the Hotel Denouement before Thursday. The only difference between us is the portraits on our uniforms."

"We're wearing Herman Melville," Klaus said. "He was a writer of enormous talent who dramatized the plight of overlooked people, such as poor sailors or exploited youngsters, through his strange, often experimental philosophical prose. I'm proud to display his portrait. But you're wearing Edgar Guest. He was a writer of limited skill, who wrote awkward, tedious poetry on hopelessly sentimental topics. You ought to be ashamed of yourself."

"Edgar Guest isn't my favorite poet," the hook-handed man admitted. "Before I joined up with Count Olaf, I was studying poetry with my stepfather. We used to read to one another in the Main Hall of the *Queequeg*. But it's too late now. I can't return to my old life."

"Maybe not," Klaus said. "But you can return us to the *Queequeg*, so we can save Sunny."

"Please," the children heard Sunny say, from inside the helmet, although her voice was quite hoarse, as if she would not be able to speak for much longer, and for a moment the only sound in the brig was Sunny's desperate coughing as the minutes in her crucial hour ticked away, and the muttering of the hook-handed man as he paced back and forth, twiddling his hooks in thought. Violet and Klaus watched his hooks, and thought of all the times he had used them to threaten the siblings. It is one thing to believe that people have both good and bad inside them, mixed together like ingredients in a salad bowl. But it is quite another to look at a cohort of a despicable villain, who has tried again and again to cause so much harm, and try to see where the good parts are buried, when all you can remember is the pain and suffering he has caused. As the hook-handed man circled the brig, it was as if the Baudelaires were picking through a chef's salad consisting mostly of dreadful—and perhaps even poisonous—ingredients, trying desperately to find the one noble crouton that might save their sister, just as I, between paragraphs, am picking through this salad in front of me, hoping that my waiter is more noble than wicked, and that my sister, Kit, might be saved by the small, herbed piece of toast I hope to retrieve from my bowl. After much hemming and hawing, however—a phrase which here means "muttering, and clearing of one's throat, used to avoid making a quick decision"—Count Olaf's henchman stopped in front of the children, put his hooks on his hips, and offered them a Hobson's choice.

"I'll return you to the *Queequeg*," he said, "if you take me with you."

Eleven

"Aye!" Fiona said. "Aye! Aye! Aye! We'll take you with us, Fernald! Aye!"

Violet and Klaus looked at one another. They were grateful, of course, that the hook-handed man was letting them save Sunny from the Medusoid Mycelium, but they couldn't help but wish Fiona had uttered fewer "Aye!"s. Inviting Count Olaf's henchman to join them on the *Queequeg*, even if he was Fiona's long-lost brother, seemed like a decision they might regret.

"I'm so glad," the hook-handed man said, giving the two siblings a smile they found inscrutable, a word which here means "either pleasant or nasty, but it was hard to tell." "I have lots of ideas about where we could go after we get off the *Carmelita*."

"Well, I'd certainly like to hear them," Fiona said. "Aye!"

"Perhaps we could discuss such things later," Violet said. "I don't think now is a good time to hesitate."

"Aye!" Fiona said. "She who hesitates is lost!"

"Or he," Klaus reminded her. "We've got to get to the *Queequeg* right away."

The hook-handed man opened the door of the brig and looked up and down the corridor. "This will be tricky," he said, beckoning to the children with one of his hooks. "The only way back to the *Queequeg* is through the rowing room, but that room is filled with children we've kidnapped. Esmé took my tagliatelle grande and is whipping them so they'll row faster."

The elder Baudelaires did not bother to point out that the hook-handed man had threatened the Baudelaires with the very same noodle, when the children had worked at Caligari Carnival, along with a few other individuals who had ended up joining Olaf's troupe. "Is there any way to sneak past them?" Violet asked.

"We'll see," Olaf's henchman said. "Follow me."

The hook-handed man strode quickly down the empty corridor, with Fiona behind him and the two Baudelaires behind her, carrying the diving helmet in which Sunny still coughed. Violet and Klaus purposefully lagged behind so they might have a word with the mycologist.

"Fiona, are you sure you want to take him with us?" Klaus asked, leaning in close to murmur in her ear. "He's a very dangerous and volatile man."

"He's my brother," Fiona replied in a fierce

whisper, "and I'm your captain. Aye! I'm in charge of the *Queequeg*, so I get to choose its crew."

"We know that," Violet said, "but we just thought you might want to reconsider."

"Never," Fiona said firmly. "With my step-father gone, Fernald may be the only person I have left in my family. Would you ask me to abandon my own sibling?"

As if replying, Sunny coughed desperately from inside her helmet, and the elder Baudelaires knew that Fiona was right. "Of course we wouldn't," Klaus said.

"Stop muttering back there," the hook-handed man ordered, as he led the children around another twist in the corridor. "We're approaching the rowing room, and we don't want anyone to hear us."

The children stopped talking, but as the henchman stopped at the door to the rowing room, and held his hook over an eye on the wall which would open the door, Violet and Klaus could hear that there was no reason to be quiet. Even through the thick metal of the rowing room entrance, they could hear the loud, piercing voice of Carmelita Spats.

"For my third dance," she was saying, "I will twirl around and around while all of you clap as hard as you can. It is a dance of celebration, in honor of the most adorable tap-dancing ballerina fairy princess veterinarian in the world!"

"Please, Carmelita," begged the voice of a child. "We've been rowing for hours. Our hands are too sore to clap."

There was a faint, damp sound, like someone dropping a washcloth, and the elder Baudelaires realized that Esmé was whipping the children with her enormous noodle. "You will participate in Carmelita's recital," the treacherous girlfriend announced, "or you will suffer the sting of my tagliatelle grande! Ha ha hoity-toity!"

"It's not really a sting," said one brave child. "It's more of a mild, wet slap."

"Shut up, cakesniffer!" Carmelita ordered,

and the children heard the rustle of her pink tutu as she began to twirl. "Start clapping!" she shrieked, and then the children heard a sound they had never heard before.

There is nothing wicked about having a dreadful singing voice, any more than there is something wicked about having dreadful posture, dreadful cousins, or a dreadful pair of pants. Many noble and pleasant people have any number of these things, and there are even one or two kind individuals who have them all. But if you have something dreadful, and you force it upon someone else, then you have done something quite wicked indeed. If you force your wicked posture on someone, for instance, by leaning so far back that they are forced to carry you down the street, then you have wickedly ruined their afternoon walk, and if you force your dreadful cousins on someone, by dropping them off to play at their house so you can escape from their dreadful presences and spend some time alone, then you have wickedly ruined their entire day, and only a very wicked person indeed would force a dreadful pair of pants on the legs and lower torso of somebody else. But to force your dreadful singing voice on somebody, or even a crowd of people, is one of the world's most wicked crimes, and at that moment Carmelita Spats opened her mouth and afflicted the crew of the *Carmelita* with her wickedness. Carmelita's singing voice was loud, like a siren, and high-pitched, like a squeaky door, and extremely off-pitch, as if all of the notes in the musical scale were pushing up against one another, all trying to sound at the same time. Her singing voice was mushy, as if someone had filled her mouth with mashed potatoes before she sang, and filled with vibrato, which is the Italian term for a voice that wavers as it sings, as if someone were shaking Carmelita very vigorously as she began her song. Even the most dreadful of voices can be tolerated if it is performing a good song, but I'm sad to say that Carmelita Spats had written the song herself and that it was just as dreadful as her singing voice. Violet and Klaus were reminded of Prufrock Preparatory School, where they had first met Carmelita. The vice principal of the school, a tedious man named Nero, forced his students to listen to him play the violin for hours, and they realized this administrator must have had a powerful influence on Carmelita's creativity.

"C is for 'cute,'" Carmelita sang,

"A is for 'adorable'!

R is for 'ravishing'!

M is for 'gorgeous'!

E is for 'excellent'!

L is for 'lovable'!

I is for 'I'm the best'!

T is for 'talented'!

and A is for 'a tap-dancing ballerina fairy princess veterinarian'!

Now let's begin my whole wonderful song all over again!"

The song was so irritating, and sung so poorly,

that Violet and Klaus almost felt as if they were being tortured after all, particularly as Carmelita kept on singing it, over and over and over.

"I can't stand her voice," Violet said. "It reminds me of the cawing of the V.F.D. crows."

"I can't stand the lyrics," Klaus said. "Someone needs to tell her that 'gorgeous' does not begin with the letter M."

"I can't stand the brat," the hook-handed man said bitterly. "She's one of the reasons I'd like to leave. But this sounds like as good a time as any to try to sneak through this room. There are plenty of pillars to hide behind, and if we walk around the very edge, where each oar sticks through the wall into the tentacles of the octopus, we should be able to get to the other door—assuming everybody is watching Carmelita's tap-dancing ballerina fairy princess veterinarian dance recital."

"That seems like a very risky plan," Violet said.

"This is no time to be a coward," the hook-handed man growled.

"My sister is not a coward," Klaus said. "She's just being cautious."

"There's no time to be cautious!" Fiona said. "Aye! She who hesitates is lost! Aye! Or he! Let's go!"

Without another word, the hook-handed man poked the eye on the wall, and the door slid open to reveal the enormous room. As Olaf's comrade had predicted, the rowing children were all facing Carmelita, who was prancing and singing on one side of the room while Esmé watched with a proud smile on her face and a large noodle in one of her tentacles. With the hook-handed man and Fiona in the lead, the three Baudelaires—Sunny still in the diving helmet, of course—made their careful way around the outside of the room as Carmelita twirled around singing her absurd song. When Carmelita announced what C was for, the children ducked behind one of the pillars. When she told her listeners the meaning of A and R, the children crept past the moving oars, taking care not to trip. When she insisted that "gorgeous" began with M, Count Olaf's henchman pointed one of his hooks at a far door, and when Carmelita reached E and L, the children ducked behind another pillar, hoping the dim light of the lanterns would not give them away. When Carmelita announced that she was the best, and bragged about being talented, Esmé Squalor frowned and turned around, blinking underneath the fake eyes of her octopus outfit, and the children had to flatten themselves on the floor so the villainous girlfriend would not spot them, and when the tap-dancing ballerina fairy princess veterinarian found it necessary to remind her audience that she was, in fact, a tap-dancing ballerina fairy princess veterinarian, the two elder Baudelaires found themselves ahead of Fiona and the hook-handed man, hiding behind a pillar that was just a few feet from their destination. They were just about to inch their way toward the door when Carmelita began belting out the last line of her song—"belting out" is a phrase which here means "singing in a particularly loud and particularly irritating voice"—only to stop herself just as she was about to begin her whole wonderful song all over again.

"C is for—cakesniffers!" she shouted. "What are you doing here?"

Violet and Klaus froze, and then saw with relief that the terrible little girl was pointing scornfully at Fiona and the hook-handed man, who were standing awkwardly between two oars.

"How dare you, Hooky?" Esmé said, fingering her large noodle as if she wanted to strike him with it. "You're interrupting a very in recital by an unspeakably darling little girl!"

"I'm very sorry, your Esméness," the hook-handed man said, stepping forward to elaborately bow in front of the wicked girlfriend. "I would sooner lose both hands all over again than interrupt Carmelita when she's dancing."

"But you *did* interrupt me, you handicapped cakesniffer!" Carmelita pouted. "Now I have to start the entire recital all over again!"

"No!" cried one of the rowing children. "Anything but that! It's torture!"

"Speaking of torture," the hook-handed man said quickly, "I stopped by to see if I could borrow your tagliatelle grande. It'll help me get the Baudelaires to reveal the location of the sugar bowl."

Esmé frowned, and fingered the noodle with one tentacle. "I don't really like to lend things," she said. "It usually leads to people messing up my stuff."

"Please, ma'am," Fiona said. "We're so close to learning the location of the sugar bowl. Aye! We just need to borrow your noodle, so we can return to the brig."

"Why are you helping Hooky?" Esmé said. "I thought you were another goody-goody orphan."

"Certainly not," the hook-handed man said. "This is my sister, Fiona, and she's joining the crew of the *Carmelita*."

"Fiona isn't a very in name," Esmé said. "I think I'll call her Triangle Eyes. Are you really willing to join us, Triangle Eyes?"

"Aye!" Fiona said. "Those Baudelaires are nothing but trouble."

"Why are you still talking?" demanded Carmelita. "This is supposed to be my special tap-dancing ballerina fairy princess veterinarian dance recital time!"

"Sorry, darling," Esmé said. "Hooky and Triangle Eyes, take this noodle and scram!"

The hook-handed man and his sister walked to the center of the room and stood directly in front of Esmé and Carmelita, offering a perfect opportunity for the elder Baudelaires to scram, a rude word which here means "slip out of the room unnoticed and walk down the shadowy hallway Olaf had led them down just a little while earlier."

"Do you think Fiona will join us?" Violet asked.

"I don't think so," Klaus said. "They told Esmé they'd return to the brig, so they'll have to go back the way we came."

"You don't think she's really joining Olaf's troupe, do you?" Violet said.

"Of course not," Klaus said. "That was just to give us an opportunity to get out of the room. Fiona may be volatile, but she's not *that* volatile."

"Of course not," Violet said, though she didn't sound very sure.

"Of course not," Klaus repeated, as another ragged cough came from inside the diving helmet. "Hang on, Sunny," he called to his sister. "You'll be cured in no time!" Although he tried to sound as confident as he could, the middle Baudelaire had no way of knowing if his words were true—although, I'm happy to say, they were.

"How are you going to cure Sunny," Violet said, "without Fiona?"

"We'll have to research it ourselves," Klaus said firmly.

"We'll never read her entire mycological library in time to make an antidote," Violet said.

"We don't have to read the entire library," Klaus said, as they reached the door to the *Queequeg*'s brig. "I know just where to look."

Sunny coughed again, and then began to wheeze, a word which here means "make a hoarse, whistling sound indicating that her throat was almost completely closed up." The elder Baudelaires could hardly stop themselves from opening the helmet to comfort their sister, but they didn't want to risk getting poisoned themselves. "I hope you're right," Violet said, pressing a metal eye on the wall. The door slid open and children hurried toward the broken porthole of the submarine. "Sunny's hour must almost be up."

Klaus nodded grimly, and jumped through the porthole onto the large wooden table. Although it had only been a short while since the children had left the *Queequeg*, the Main Hall felt as if it had been abandoned for years. The three balloons tied to the table legs were beginning to sag, the tidal charts Klaus had studied had fallen to the floor, and the glass circle Count Olaf had cut in the porthole still lay on the floor. But the middle Baudelaire ignored all of these objects, and picked up *Mushroom Minutiae* from the floor.

"This book should have information on the antidote," he said, and turned immediately to the table of contents as Violet carried Sunny through the porthole into the submarine. "Chapter Thirty-Six, The Yeast of Beasts. Chapter Thirty-Seven, Morel Behavior in a Free Society. Chapter Thirty-Eight, Fungible Mold, Moldable Fungi. Chapter Thirty-Nine, Visitable Fungal Ditches. Chapter Forty, The Gorgonian Grotto."

"That's it!" Violet said. "Chapter Forty."

Klaus flipped pages as Sunny gave another desperate wheeze, although I wish the middle

Baudelaire could have had the time to return to some of those pages he flipped past. "'The Gorgonian Grotto,'" he read, "'located in propinquity to Anwhistle Aquatics, has appropriately wraithlike nomenclature—'"

"We know all that," Violet said hurriedly. "Skip to the part about the mycelium."

Klaus's eyes scanned the page easily, having had much practice in skipping the parts of books he found less than helpful. "'The Medusoid Mycelium has a unique conducive strategy of waxing—'"

"'And waning,'" interrupted Violet, as Sunny's wheezing continued to wax. "Skip to the part about the poison."

"'As the poet says,'" Klaus read, "'A single spore has such grim power/That you may die within the hour. Is dilution simple? But of course!/Just one small dose of root of horse.'"

"'Root of horse'?" Violet repeated. "How can a horse have a root?"

"I don't know," Klaus said. "Usually antidotes are certain botanical extractions, like pollen from a flower, or the stem of a plant."

"Does 'dilution' mean the same thing as 'antidote'?" Violet asked, but before her brother could answer, Sunny wheezed again, and the diving helmet rocked back and forth as she struggled against the fungus. Klaus looked at the book he was holding, and then at his sister, and then reached into the waterproof pocket of his uniform.

"What are you doing?" Violet asked.

"Getting my commonplace book," Klaus replied. "I wrote down all the information on the history of Anwhistle Aquatics that we found in the grotto."

"We don't have time to look at your research!" Violet said. "We need to find an antidote this very minute! Fiona's right—He or she who hesitates is lost."

Klaus shook his head. "Not necessarily," he said, and flipped a page of his dark blue notebook. "If we take one moment to think, we might save our sister. Now, what did Kit Snicket write in that letter? Here it is: 'The poisonous fungus you insist on cultivating in the grotto will bring grim consequences for all of us. Our factory at Lousy Lane can provide some dilution of the mycelium's destructive respiratory capabilities. . . .' That's it! V.F.D. was making something in a factory near Lousy Lane that could dilute the effects of the mycelium."

"Lousy Lane?" Violet said. "That was the road to Uncle Monty's house. It had a terrible smell, remember? It smelled like black pepper. No, not black pepper. . ."

Klaus looked at his commonplace book, and then at *Mushroom Minutiae.* "Horseradish," he said quietly. "The road smelled like horseradish! 'Root of horse'! Horseradish is the antidote!"

Violet was already striding to the kitchen. "Let's hope Phil likes to cook with horseradish," she said, and pushed open the door. Klaus picked up the wheezing helmet and followed her into the tiny kitchen. There was scarcely enough room for the children to stand in the small space between the stove, the refrigerator, and two wooden cabinets.

"The cabinets must serve as a pantry," Klaus said, using a word which here means "place where antidotes are hopefully stored." "Horseradish should be there—if he has it."

The elder Baudelaires shuddered, not wanting to think about what would happen to Sunny if horseradish were not found on the shelves. Within moments, however, Violet and Klaus had to consider that very thing. Violet opened one cupboard, and Klaus opened another, but the children saw immediately that there was no horseradish. "Gum," Violet said faintly. "Boxes and boxes of gum Phil brought from the lumbermill, and nothing else. Did you find anything, Klaus?"

Klaus pointed to a pair of small cans on one shelf of his cupboard, and held up a small paper bag. "Two cans of water chestnuts," he said, "and a small bag of sesame seeds." His fist closed tightly around the bag, and he blinked back tears behind his glasses. "What are we going to do?"

Sunny wheezed once more, a frantic whistle that reminded her siblings of a train's lonely noise as it disappears into a tunnel. "Let's check the refrigerator," Violet said. "Maybe there's horseradish in there."

Klaus nodded, and opened the kitchen's refrigerator, which was almost as bare as the pantry. On the top shelf were six small bottles of lemon-lime soda, which Phil had offered the children on their first night aboard the *Queequeg*. On the middle shelf was a small piece of white, soft cheese, wrapped up in a bit of wax paper. And on the bottom shelf was a large plate, on which was something that made the two siblings begin to cry.

"I forgot," Violet said, tears running down her face.

"Me too," Klaus said, taking the plate out of the refrigerator.

Phil had used the last of the kitchen's pro-
visions—a word which here means "cooking
supplies"—to prepare a cake. It looked like a
coconut cream cake, like Dr. Montgomery used
to make, and the two siblings wondered if
Sunny, even as a baby, had noticed enough
about cooking to help Phil concoct such a
dessert. The cake was heavily frosted, with bits
of coconut mixed into the thick, creamy frosting, and spelled out in blue frosting on the top,
in Phil's perky, optimistic handwriting, were
three words.

"Violet's Fifteenth Date," Klaus said
numbly. "That's what the balloons were for."

"It was my fifteenth birthday," Violet said.
"I turned fifteen sometime when we were in the
grotto, and I forgot all about it."

"Sunny didn't forget," Klaus said. "She said
she was planning a surprise, remember? We
were going to return from our mission in the
cave, and celebrate your birthday."

Violet slunk to the floor, and lay her head

against Sunny's diving helmet. "What are we going to do?" she sobbed. "We can't lose Sunny. We can't lose her!"

"There must be something we can use," Klaus said, "as a substitute for horseradish. What could it be?"

"I don't know!" Violet cried. "I don't know anything about cooking!"

"Neither do I!" Klaus said, crying as hard as his sister. "Sunny's the one who knows!"

The two weeping Baudelaires looked at one another, and then steeled themselves, a phrase which here means "summoned up as much strength as they could." Then, without another word, they opened the tiny door of Sunny's helmet and quickly dragged their sister out, quickly shutting the door behind her so the fungus would not spread. At first, their sister looked completely unchanged, but when the wheezing young girl opened her mouth, they could see several gray stalks and caps of this horrible mushroom, splotched with black as if someone had poured ink into Sunny's mouth. Wheezing horribly, Sunny reached out her tiny arms to each of her siblings and grabbed their hands. She did not have to utter a word. Violet and Klaus knew she was begging for help, but there was nothing they could do except ask her one desperate question.

"Sunny," Violet said, "we've researched an antidote. Only horseradish can save you. But there's no horseradish in the kitchen."

"Sunny," Klaus said, "is there a culinary equivalent of horseradish?"

Sunny opened her mouth as if trying to say something, but the elder Baudelaires only heard the hoarse, whistling sound of air trying to make its way past the mushrooms. Her tiny hands curled into fists, and her body twisted back and forth in pain and fear. Finally, she managed to utter one word—a word that many might not have understood. Some might have thought it was part of Sunny's personal vocabulary—perhaps her way of saying "I love you," or even

"Farewell, siblings." Some might have thought it was pure nonsense, just the noises one might make when a deadly fungus has defeated you. But there are many others who would have understood it immediately. A person from Japan would have known she was talking about a condiment often served with raw fish and pickled ginger. A chef would have known that Sunny was referring to a strong, green root, widely considered the culinary equivalent of horseradish. And Violet and Klaus knew that their sister was naming her salvation, a phrase which here means "something that would save her life," or "something that would rescue her from the Medusoid Mycelium," or, most importantly, "an item the eldest Baudelaire still had in the water-proof pocket of her uniform, sealed in a tin Sunny had found in an underwater cavern."

"Wasabi," Sunny said, in a hoarse, mushroom-choked whisper, and she did not have to say anything more.

CHAPTER

Twelve

The expression "the tables have turned" is not one the Baudelaire orphans had much occasion to use, as it refers to a situation that has suddenly been reversed, so that those who were previously in a powerless position could suddenly find themselves in a powerful one, and vice versa. For the Baudelaires, the tables had turned at Briny Beach, when they received news of the terrible fire, and Count Olaf suddenly became a powerful and terrifying figure in their lives. As time went on, the siblings waited and waited for the tables to turn back, so that Olaf might be defeated once and for all and they could find themselves free of the sinister and mysterious forces that threatened to engulf them, but the tables of the Baudelaires' lives seemed stuck, with the children always in a position of misery and sorrow while wickedness seemed to triumph all around them. But as Violet hurriedly opened the tin of wasabi she had been keeping in her pocket, and spooned the green, spicy mixture into Sunny's wheezing mouth, it seemed like the tables might turn after all. Sunny gasped when the wasabi hit her tongue, and the stalks and caps of the Medusoid Mycelium shivered, and seemed to shrink back from the powerful Japanese condiment. In moments, the fungus began to wither and fade away, and Sunny's wheezing faded into coughing, and her coughing faded into deep breaths as the youngest Baudelaire rallied, a word which here means "regained her strength, and ability to breathe." The youngest Baudelaire hung on tight to her siblings' hands, and her eyes filled with tears, but Violet and Klaus could see that the Medusoid Mycelium would not triumph over their sister.

"It's working," Violet said. "Sunny's breathing is getting stronger."

"Yes," Klaus said. "We've turned the tables on that ghastly fungus."

"Water," Sunny said, and her brother stood up from the kitchen floor and quickly got his sister a glass of water. Weakly, the youngest Baudelaire sat up and drank deeply from the glass, and then hugged both her siblings as tightly as she could.

"Thank you," she said. "Saved me."

"You saved yourself," Violet pointed out. "We had the wasabi this whole time, but we didn't think of giving it to you until you told us."

Sunny coughed again, and lay back down on the floor. "Tuckered," she murmured.

"I'm not surprised you're exhausted," Violet

said. "You've been through quite an ordeal. Shall we carry you to the barracks so you can rest?"

"Rest here," Sunny said, curling up at the foot of the stove.

"Will you really be comfortable on the kitchen floor?" Klaus asked.

Sunny opened one exhausted eye and smiled at her siblings. "Near you," she said.

"All right, Sunny," Violet said, grabbing a dish towel from the kitchen counter, and folding it into a pillow for her sister. "We'll be in the Main Hall if you need us."

"What next?" she murmured.

"Shh," Klaus said, putting another dish towel on top of her. "Don't worry, Sunny. We'll figure out what to do next."

The Baudelaires tiptoed out of the kitchen, carrying the tin of wasabi. "Do you think she'll be all right?" Violet asked.

"I'm sure she will," Klaus said. "After a nap she'll be as good as new. But we should eat some of that wasabi ourselves. When we opened the diving helmet, we were exposed to the Medusoid Mycelium, and we'll need all of our strength to get away from Olaf."

Violet nodded, and put a spoonful of wasabi into her mouth, shuddering violently as the condiment hit her tongue. "There's one last spoonful," Violet said, handing the tin to her brother. "We'd better make sure that diving helmet stays closed until we get our hands on some horseradish and destroy that fungus for good."

Klaus nodded in agreement, closed his eyes, and ate the last of the Japanese condiment. "If we ever invent that food code we talked about with Fiona," he said, "the word 'wasabi' should mean 'powerful.' No wonder this cured our sister."

"But now that we've cured her," Violet said, remembering Sunny's question as she fell asleep, "what next?"

"Olaf is next," Klaus said firmly. "He said he has everything he needs to defeat V.F.D.

forever—except the sugar bowl."

"You're right," Violet said. "We have to turn the tables on him, and find it before he does."

"But we don't know where it is," Klaus said. "Someone must have taken it from the Gorgonian Grotto."

"I wonder—" Violet said, but she never said what she wondered, because a strange noise interrupted her. The noise was a sort of whir, followed by a sort of beep, followed by all sorts of noises, and they seemed to be coming from deep within the machinery of the *Queequeg*. Finally, a green light lit up on a panel in the wall, and a flat, white object began to slither out of a tiny slit in the panel.

"It's paper," Klaus said.

"It's more than paper," Violet said, and walked over to the panel. The sheet of paper curled into her hand as it emerged from the slit, as if the machine were impatient for the eldest Baudelaire to read it. "This is the telegram device. We must be receiving—"

"A Volunteer Factual Dispatch," Klaus finished.

Violet nodded, and scanned the paper quickly. Sure enough, the words "Volunteer Factual Dispatch" were printed on the top, and as more and more of the paper appeared, the eldest Baudelaire saw that it was addressed "To the *Queequeg*," with the date printed below, as well as the name of the person who was sending the telegram, miles and miles away on dry land. It was a name Violet almost dared not say out loud, even though she had felt as if she had been whispering it to herself for days, ever since the icy waters of the Stricken Stream had carried away a young man who meant very much to her.

"It's from Quigley Quagmire," she said quietly.

Klaus's eyes widened in astonishment. "What does he say?" he asked.

Violet smiled as the telegram finished printing, her finger touching the Q in her friend's name. It was almost as if knowing that

Quigley was alive was enough of a message. "'It is my understanding that you have three additional volunteers on board STOP,'" she read, remembering that "STOP" indicates the end of a sentence in a telegram. "'We are in desperate need of their services for a most urgent matter STOP. Please deliver them Tuesday to the location indicated in the rhymes below STOP.'" She scanned the paper and frowned thoughtfully. "Then there are two poems," she said. "One by Lewis Carroll and the other by T. S. Eliot."

Klaus took his commonplace book out of his pocket, and flipped pages until he found what he was looking for. "Verse Fluctuation Declaration," he said. "That's the code we learned in the grotto. Quigley must have changed some of the words in the poems, so no one else would know where we're supposed to meet him. Let's see if we can recognize the changes."

Violet nodded, and read the first poem out loud:

"'O Oysters, come and walk with us!'
The Walrus did beseech.
'A pleasant walk, a pleasant talk,
Along the movie theater.'"

"That last part sounds wrong," Violet said.

"There were no movie theaters when Lewis Carroll was alive," Klaus said. "But what are the real words to the poem?"

"I don't know," Violet said. "I've always found Lewis Carroll too whimsical for my taste."

"I like him," Klaus said, "but I haven't memorized his poems. Read the other one. Maybe that will help."

Violet nodded, and read aloud:

"At the pink hour, when the eyes and back
Turn upward from the desk, when the human engine waits
Like a pony throbbing party . . ."

The voice of the eldest Baudelaire trailed

off, and she looked at her brother in confusion. "That's all," she said. "The poem stops there."

Klaus frowned. "There's nothing else in the telegram?"

"Only a few letters at the very bottom," she said. "'CC: J.S.' What does that mean?"

"'CC' means that Quigley sent a copy of this message to someone else," Klaus said, "and 'J.S.' are the initials of the person."

"Those mysterious initials again," Violet said. "It can't be Jacques Snicket, because he's dead. But who else could it be?"

"We can't worry about that now," Klaus said. "We have to figure out what words have been substituted in these poems."

"How can we do that?" Violet asked.

"I don't know," Klaus said. "Why would Quigley think we would have memorized these poems?"

"He wouldn't think that," Violet said. "He knows us. But the telegram was addressed to the *Queequeg*. He knew that someone on board could decode the poetry."

"But who?" Klaus asked. "Not Fiona—she's a mycologist. An optimist like Phil isn't likely to be familiar with T. S. Eliot. And it's hard to imagine Captain Widdershins having a serious interest in poetry."

"Not anymore," Violet said thoughtfully. "But Fiona's brother said he and the captain used to study poetry together."

"That's true," Klaus said. "He said they used to read to one another in the Main Hall." He walked over to the sideboard and opened the cabinet, peering at the books Fiona kept inside. "But there's no poetry here—just Fiona's mycological library."

"Captain Widdershins wouldn't keep poetry books out front like that," Violet said. "He would have kept them secret."

"Just like he kept the secret of what happened to Fiona's brother," Klaus said.

"He thought there were secrets too terrible for young people to know," Violet said, "but now we need to know them."

Klaus was silent for a moment, and then turned to his sister. "There's something I never told you," he said. "Remember when our parents were so angry over the spoiled atlas?"

"We talked about that in the grotto," Violet said. "The rain spoiled it when we left the library window open."

"I don't think that's the only reason they were mad," Klaus said. "I took that atlas down from the top shelf—one I could only reach by putting the stepladder on top of the chair. They didn't think I could reach that shelf."

"Why would that make them angry?" Violet asked.

Klaus looked down. "That's where they kept books they didn't want us to find," he said. "I was interested in the atlas, but when I removed it from the shelf there was a whole row of other books."

"What kind of books?" Violet asked.

"I didn't get a good look at them," Klaus asked. "There were a few books about war, and I think a few romances. I was too interested in the atlas to investigate any further, but I remember thinking it was strange that our parents had hidden those books. That's why they were so angry, I think—when they saw the atlas on the window seat, they knew I'd discovered their secret."

"Did you ever look at them again?" Violet said.

"I didn't have a chance," Klaus said. "They moved them to another hiding place, and I never saw them again."

"Maybe our parents were going to tell us what was in those books when we were older," Violet said.

"Maybe," Klaus agreed. "But we'll never know. We lost them in the fire."

The elder Baudelaires sat quietly for a moment, looking at the cabinet in the sideboard, and then, without a word, the two siblings stepped onto the wooden table so they could open the highest cabinet. Inside was a small stack of books on such dull topics as child rearing, proper and improper diets, and the water cycle, but when the children pushed these books aside they saw what they had been looking for.

"Elizabeth Bishop," Violet said, "Charles Simic, Samuel Taylor Coleridge, Franz Wright, Daphne Gottlieb—there's all sorts of poetry here."

"Why don't you read T. S. Eliot," Klaus suggested, handing her a thick, dusty volume, "and I'll tackle Lewis Carroll. If we read quickly we should be able to find the real poems and decode the message."

"I found something else," Violet said, handing her brother a crumpled square of paper. "Look."

Klaus looked at what his sister had given him. It was a photograph, blurred and faded with age, of four people, grouped together like a family. In the center of the photograph was a large man with a long mustache that was curved at the end like a pair of parentheses—Captain Widdershins, of course, although he looked much younger and a great deal happier than the children had ever seen him. He was laughing, and his arm was around someone the two Baudelaires recognized as the hook-handed man, although he was not hook-handed in the photograph—both of his hands were perfectly intact, one resting on the captain's shoulder, and the other pointing at whoever was taking the picture—and he was young enough to still be called a teenager, instead of a man. On the other side of the captain was a woman who was laughing as hard as the captain, and in her arms was a young infant with a tiny set of triangular glasses.

"That must be Fiona's mother," Klaus said, pointing at the laughing woman.

"Look," Violet said, pointing to the wall behind the family. "This was taken on board the *Queequeg*. That's the edge of the plaque with the captain's personal philosophy—'He who hesitates is lost.'"

"The whole family is lost, almost," Klaus said quietly. "Fiona's mother is dead. Her brother joined Count Olaf's troupe. And who knows where her stepfather is?" He put down the photograph, opened his commonplace book, and flipped to the beginning, where he had pasted another photograph taken long ago. This photograph also had four people in it, although one of the people was facing away from the camera, so it was impossible to tell who it was. The second person was Jacques Snicket, who of course was long dead. And the other two people were the Baudelaire parents. Klaus had kept this photograph ever since the children found it at Heimlich Hospital, and had looked at it every day, gazing into his parents' faces and reading the one sentence, over and over, that had been typed below it. "Because of the evidence discussed on page nine," the sentence read, "experts now suspect that there may in fact be one survivor of the fire, but the survivor's whereabouts are unknown." For quite some time, the Baudelaires had thought this meant one of their parents was alive after all, but now they were almost certain it meant no such thing. Violet and Klaus looked from one photograph to the other, imagining a time when no one in the pictures was lost, and everyone was happy.

Klaus sighed, and looked at his sister. "Maybe we shouldn't be hesitating here," Klaus said. "Maybe we should be rescuing our captain, instead of reading books of poetry and looking at old photographs. I don't want to lose Fiona."

"Fiona's safe with her brother," Violet said, "and I'm sure she'll join us when she can. We need to decode this message, or we might lose everything. In this case, he or she who doesn't hesitate is lost."

"What if we decode the message before Fiona arrives?" Klaus asked. "Do we wait for her to join us?"

"We wouldn't have to," Violet said. "The three of us could properly operate this submarine by ourselves. All we'd need to do is repair the porthole, and we could probably steer the *Queequeg* out of the *Carmelita*."

"We can't abandon her here," Klaus said. "She wouldn't abandon us."

"Are you sure?" Violet asked.

Klaus sighed, and looked at the photograph again. "No," he said. "Let's get to work."

Violet nodded in agreement, and the two Baudelaires shelved the discussion—a phrase which here means "temporarily stopped their conversation"—and unshelved the poetry books in order to get to work on decoding Quigley's Verse Fluctuation Declarations. It had been some time since the Baudelaires had been able to read in a comfortable place, and the children were pleased to find themselves silently flipping pages, searching for certain words, and even taking a few notes. Reading poetry, even if you are only reading to find a secret message hidden within its words, can often give one a feeling of power, the way you can feel powerful if you are the only one who brought an umbrella on a rainy day, or the only one who knows how to untie knots when you're taken hostage. With each poem the children felt more and more power-ful—or, as they might have said in their food code, more and more wasabi—and by the time the two volunteers were interrupted they felt as if the tables just might be continuing to turn.

"Snack!" announced a cheerful voice below them, and Violet and Klaus were pleased to see their sister emerging from the kitchen carrying a small plate.

"Sunny!" Violet cried. "We thought you were asleep."

"Rekoop," the youngest Baudelaire said, which meant something along the lines of, "I had a brief nap, and when I woke up I felt well enough to cook something."

"I am a bit hungry," Klaus admitted. "What did you make us?"

"Amuse bouche," Sunny said, which meant something like, "Tiny water chestnut sandwiches, with a spread of cheese and sesame seeds."

"They're quite tasty," Violet said, and the three children shared the plate of amuse bouche as the elder Baudelaires brought Sunny up to speed, a phrase which here means "told their sister what had happened while she was suffering inside the diving helmet." They told her about the terrible submarine that had swallowed the *Queequeg*, and the terrible villain they encountered inside. They described the hideous circumstances in which the Snow Scouts found themselves, and the hideous clothing worn by Esmé Squalor and Carmelita Spats. They told her about the Volunteer Factual Dispatch, and the Verse Fluctuation Declarations they were trying to decode. And, finally, they told her about the hook-handed man being Fiona's long-lost brother, and the possibility that he might join them aboard the *Queequeg*.

"Perifido," Sunny said, which meant "It would be foolish to trust one of Olaf's henchmen."

"We don't trust him," Klaus said. "Not really. But Fiona trusts him, and we trust Fiona."

"Volatile," Sunny said.

"Yes," Violet admitted, "but we don't have much choice. We're in the middle of the ocean—"

"And we need to get to the beach," Klaus said, and held up the book of Lewis Carroll's poetry. "I think I've solved part of the Verse Fluctuation Declaration. Lewis Carroll has a poem called 'The Walrus and the Carpenter.'"

"There was something about a walrus in the telegram," Violet said.

"Yes," Klaus said. "It took me a while to find the specific stanza, but here it is. Quigley wrote:

"'*O Oysters, come and walk with us!*'
The Walrus did beseech.
'*A pleasant walk, a pleasant talk,*
Along the movie theater.'"

"Yes," Violet said. "But what does the actual poem say?"

Klaus read,

"'O Oysters, come and walk with us!'
The Walrus did beseech.
'A pleasant walk, a pleasant talk,
Along the briny beach.'"

Klaus closed the book and looked up at his sisters. "Quigley wants us to meet him tomorrow," he said, "at Briny Beach."

"Briny Beach," Violet repeated quietly. The eldest Baudelaire did not have to remind her siblings, of course, of the last time they were at Briny Beach, learning from Mr. Poe that the tables of their lives had turned. The three siblings sat and thought of that terrible day, which felt as blurred and faded as the photograph of Fiona's family—or the photograph of their own parents, pasted into Klaus's commonplace book. Returning to Briny Beach after all this time felt to the Baudelaires like an enormous step backward, as if they would lose their parents and their home again, and Mr. Poe would take them once more to Count Olaf's house, and all the unfortunate events would crash over them once more, like the waves of the ocean crashing on the tidepools of Briny Beach and the tiny, passive creatures who lived inside them.

"How would we get there?" Klaus asked.

"In the *Queequeg*," Violet said. "This submarine should have a location device, and once we know where we are, I think I could set a course for Briny Beach."

"Distance?" Sunny asked.

"It shouldn't be far," Klaus said. "I'd have to check the charts. But what would we do when we got there?"

"I think I have the answer to that," Violet said, turning to her book of T. S. Eliot poems. "Quigley used lines from a very long poem in this book called *The Waste Land*."

"I tried to read that," Klaus said, "but I found

T. S. Eliot too opaque. I scarcely understood a word."

"Maybe it's all in code," Violet said. "Listen to this. Quigley wrote:

"At the pink hour, when the eyes and back
Turn upward from the desk, when the human engine waits
Like a pony throbbing party . . .

"But the real poem reads

"At the violet hour, when the eyes and back
Turn upward from the desk, when the human engine waits
Like a—"

"Blah blah blah ha ha ha!" interrupted a cruel, mocking voice. "Ha blah ha blah ha blah! Tee hee snaggle sniggle tee hee hee! Hubba hubba giggle diddle denouement!"

The Baudelaires looked up from their books

to face Count Olaf, who was already stepping through the porthole and onto the wooden table. Behind him was Esmé Squalor, sneering beneath the hood of her octopus outfit, and the children could hear the unpleasant slapping footsteps of the horrid pink shoes of Carmelita Spats, who peeked her heart-decorated face into the submarine and giggled nastily.

"I'm happier than a pig eating bacon!" Count Olaf cried. "I'm tickled pinker than a sunburned Caucasian! I'm in higher spirits than a brand-new graveyard! I'm so happy-go-lucky that lucky and happy people are going to beat me with sticks out of pure, unbridled jealousy! Ha ha jicama! When I stopped by the brig to see how my associate was progressing, and found that you orphans had flown the coop, I was afraid you were escaping, or sabotaging my submarine, or even sending a telegram asking for help! But I should have known you were too dim-witted to do anything useful! Look at yourselves, orphans, snacking and reading poetry, while the powerful and good-looking people of the world cackle in triumph! Cackle cackle cutthroat!"

"In just a few minutes," Esmé bragged, "we will arrive at the Hotel Denouement, thanks to our bratty rowing crew. Tee hee triumphant! V.F.D.'s last safe place will soon be in ashes— just like your home, Baudelaires!"

"I'm going to do a special tap-dancing ballerina fairy princess veterinarian dance recital," Carmelita bragged, "on the graves of all those volunteers!" Carmelita leaped through the porthole, her pink tutu fluttering as if it were trying to escape, and joined Olaf on the table to begin a dance of triumph.

"*C is for 'cute,'*" Carmelita sang,
  A is for 'adorable'!
  R is for 'ravishing'!
  M is for 'gor—'"

"Now, now, Carmelita," Count Olaf said, giving the tap-dancing ballerina fairy princess veterinarian a tense smile. "Why don't you save your dance recital for later? I'll buy you all the dance costumes in the world. With V.F.D. out of the way, all the fortunes of the world can be mine—the Baudelaire fortune, the Quagmire fortune, the Widdershins fortune, the—"

"Where is Fiona?" Klaus asked, interrupting the villain. "What have you done with her? If you've hurt her—"

"Hurt her?" Count Olaf asked, his eyes shining bright beneath his one scraggly eyebrow. "Hurt Triangle Eyes? Why would I hurt a clever girl like that? Tee hee troupe member!"

With one of his tiresome dramatic gestures, Count Olaf pointed behind him, and Esmé clapped the tentacles of her outfit as two people appeared in the porthole. One was the hook-handed man, who looked as wicked as he ever had. And the other was Fiona, who looked slightly different. One difference was the expression on her face, which looked resigned, a word which here means "as if the mycologist had given up entirely on defeating Count Olaf." But the other difference was printed on the slippery-looking uniform she was wearing, right in the center.

"No," Klaus said quietly, as he stared at his friend.

"No," Violet said firmly, and looked at Klaus.

"No!" Sunny said angrily, and bared her teeth as Fiona stepped through the porthole and stood beside Count Olaf on the wooden table. Her boot brushed against the poetry books Violet and Klaus had taken from the sideboard, including books by Lewis Carroll and T. S. Eliot. There are some who say that the poetry of Lewis Carroll is too whimsical, a word which here means "full of comic nonsense," and other people complain that T. S. Eliot's poetry is too opaque, which refers to something that is unnecessarily complicated. But while everyone may not agree on the poets represented on the wooden table, every noble reader in the world agrees that the poet represented on Fiona's uniform was a writer of limited skill, who wrote awkward, tedious poetry on hopelessly sentimental topics.

"Yes," Fiona said quietly, and the Baudelaire orphans looked up at the portrait of Edgar Guest, smiling on the front of her uniform, and felt the tables turn once more.

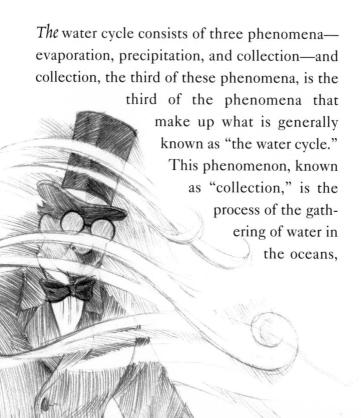

The water cycle consists of three phenomena—
evaporation, precipitation, and collection—and
collection, the third of these phenomena, is the
third of the phenomena that
make up what is generally
known as "the water cycle."
This phenomenon, known
as "collection," is the
process of the gath-
ering of water in
the oceans,

lakes, rivers, ponds, reservoirs, and puddles of the world, so that it will eventually go through the phenomena of evaporation and precipitation, thus beginning the water cycle all over again. It is a tedious thing for a reader to find in a book, of course, and I hope that my descriptions of the water cycle have bored you enough that you have put this book down long ago, and will not read Chapter Thirteen of *The Grim Grotto* any more than the Baudelaire orphans will ever read Chapter Thirty-Nine of *Mushroom Minutiae*, no matter how crucial such a chapter might be. But however tedious the water cycle is to readers, it must be very tedious indeed to the drops of water who must participate in the cycle over and over again. Occasionally, when I pause while writing my chronicle of the Baudelaire orphans, and my eyes and back turn upward from my desk to look out at the evening sky—the purple color of which explains the expression "the violet hour"—I imagine myself as a drop of water, especially if it is raining, or if my desk is floating in a reservoir. I think of how ghastly it would feel to be yanked away from my comrades, when we were gathered in a lake or puddle, and forced into the sky through the process of evaporation. I think how terrible it would feel to be chased out of a cloud by the process of precipitation, and tumble to the earth like a sugar bowl. And I think of how heartbroken I would feel to gather once more in a body of water and feel, during the process of collection, that I had reached the last safe place, only to have the tables turn, and evaporate into the sky once more as the tedious cycle started all over again. It is awful to contemplate this sort of life, in which one would always be forced into motion by a variety of mysterious and powerful forces, never staying anywhere for long, never finding a safe place one could call home, never able to turn the tables for very long, just as the Baudelaire orphans found it awful to contemplate their own lives as Fiona betrayed them, as so many of their companions had betrayed them before, just when it seemed they might break out of the tedious cycle of unfortunate events in which they found themselves trapped.

"Tell them, Triangle Eyes," Count Olaf said with a wicked smile. "Tell the Baudelaires that you've joined up with me."

"It's true," Fiona said, but behind her triangular glasses her eyes were downcast, a word which here means "looking sadly at the floor." "Count Olaf said that if I helped him destroy the last safe place, he'd help me find my stepfather."

"But Count Olaf and your stepfather are enemies!" Violet cried. "They're on opposite sides of the schism."

"I wouldn't be so sure about that," Esmé Squalor said, her suction cups dragging along the floor as she stepped through the broken porthole. "After all, Captain Widdershins abandoned you. Maybe he's decided volunteers are out—and we're in."

"My brother, my stepfather, and I could be together again," Fiona said quietly. "Don't you understand, Baudelaires?"

"Of course they don't understand!" Count Olaf cried. "Ha ha half-wits! Those brats spend their lives reading books instead of chasing after fortunes! Now, let's remove all the valuables from the *Queequeg* and we'll lock the orphans up in the brig!"

"You won't get away from us this time!" the hook-handed man said, taking the tagliatelle grande from behind his back and whirling the noodle in the air.

"We didn't get away from you last time," Klaus said. "You helped us sneak over here, to save Sunny. You said you wanted to come with us when we escaped in the *Queequeg* and joined V.F.D. at the last safe place."

"V.F.D.," the hook-handed man sneered. With one scornful flick of his hook he popped one of the balloons Phil had used to decorate the Main Hall for Violet's birthday. "All those silly volunteers with their precious libraries and complicated codes—they're fools, every last one of them. I don't want to sit around reading idiotic books! He who hesitates is lost!"

"Or she," Fiona said. "Aye!"

"Yes," Count Olaf said, "let's not hesitate a moment longer, Hooky. Let's tour this submarine and steal anything we want!"

"I want to come, too!" Esmé said. "I need a new fashionable outfit!"

"Of course, boss," the hook-handed man said, walking toward the door of the Main Hall. "Follow me."

"No, you follow *me*!" Count Olaf said, pushing ahead of him. "I'm in charge!"

"But Countie," Carmelita whined, jumping off the wooden table and twirling around awkwardly. "I want to go first because I'm a tap-dancing ballerina fairy princess veterinarian!"

"Of course you get to go first, precious," Esmé said. "You get whatever your adorable little heart desires, right Olaf?"

"I guess so," Olaf muttered.

"And tell Triangle Eyes to stay here and guard the orphans," Carmelita said. "I don't want her to take all the good stuff for herself."

"Guard the orphans, Triangle Eyes," Count Olaf said. "Although I don't think you orphans really need to be guarded. After all, there's nowhere for you to go! Tee hee traction!"

"Giggle giggle gaudy!" Carmelita cried, leading the way out of the Main Hall.

"Ha ha hair trigger!" Esmé screamed, following her.

"Tee hee tonsillectomy!" Count Olaf shrieked, walking behind his girlfriend.

"I also find this amusing!" the hook-handed man yelled, and slammed the door behind him, leaving the Baudelaires alone with Fiona.

"Traitor," Sunny said.

"Sunny's right," Violet said. "Don't do this, Fiona. There's still time to change your mind, and stay on the noble side of the schism."

"We received a Volunteer Factual Dispatch,"

Klaus said, holding up the telegram. "V.F.D. is in desperate need of our services for a most urgent matter. We're meeting the volunteers at Briny Beach. You could come with us, Fiona."

"Greenhut!" Sunny cried. She meant something like, "You could be of enormous help," but Fiona didn't even wait for a translation.

"You wouldn't abandon your sister," the mycologist said. "Aye! You risked your lives to save Sunny. How can you ask me to abandon my brother?"

"Your brother is a wicked person," Violet said.

"People aren't either wicked or noble," Fiona said. "They're like chef's salads."

Klaus picked up the photograph from the table and handed it to Fiona. "This doesn't look like a chef's salad to me," he said. "It looks like a family. Is this what your family would have you do, Fiona? Send three children to the brig, while you help a villain in his treacherous schemes?"

Fiona looked at the picture, and blinked

back tears behind her triangular glasses. "My family is lost," she said. "Aye! My mother is dead. Aye! My father moved away. Aye! My stepfather has abandoned me. Aye! My brother may not be as wonderful as you Baudelaires, but he is the only family I have. Aye! I'm staying with him. Aye!"

"Stay with him if you must," Violet said, "but let us go."

"Rendezvous," Sunny said.

"Take us to Briny Beach," Klaus translated. "We might be on opposite sides of the schism, Fiona, but that doesn't mean we can't help one another."

Fiona sighed, and looked first at the Baudelaires and then at the photograph of her family. "I could turn my back," she said, "instead of guarding you."

"And we could take the *Queequeg*," Violet said, "and escape."

Fiona frowned, and put the photograph back down on the table. "If I let you go to Briny

Beach," she said, "what will you do for me?"

"I'll teach you how to repair submarines," Violet said, gesturing to the telegram device. "You could restore the *Queequeg* to its former glory."

"I don't need the *Queequeg* anymore," Fiona said. "Aye! I'm part of the crew of the *Carmelita*."

"I'll give you my commonplace book," Klaus said, holding out his dark blue notebook. "It's full of important secrets."

"Count Olaf knows more secrets than you'll ever learn," Fiona replied.

"Mmph!" The children looked down and saw Sunny, who had slipped away while the others were talking, and was now walking unsteadily back through the door marked KITCHEN, dragging her diving helmet.

"Don't touch that, Sunny!" Violet cried. "There's a very dangerous fungus in there, and we don't have any more antidote!"

"Mycolo," Sunny said, and lay the helmet at Fiona's feet.

"Sunny's right," Klaus said, looking at the helmet and shuddering. "Inside that helmet is the bugaboo of the mycological pantheon—the Medusoid Mycelium."

"I thought you destroyed it," Fiona said.

"No," Violet said. "The Medusoid Mycelium grows best in an enclosed space. You said that the poison of a deadly fungus can be the source of some wonderful medicines. This is a very valuable specimen for a mycologist like yourself."

"That's true," Fiona admitted quietly, and looked down at the helmet. The Baudelaires looked down, too, remembering their terrible journey through the grotto. They remembered how cold and dark it was when they left the *Queequeg* and drifted through the cavern, and the horrifying sight of the Medusoid Mycelium trapping them in the eerie cave until the stalks and caps waned away. They remembered their chilly journey back to the submarine, and the dreadful discoveries of the missing crew and the mushrooms sprouting inside Sunny's helmet, and the image of the octopus submarine on the sonar screen, and the villain who was waiting for them when they tumbled inside.

"We're back!" Count Olaf announced, bursting back into the Main Hall with his comrades behind him. Esmé and Carmelita were peeking into a small, shiny box, and the hook-handed man was staggering under the weight of the uniforms and diving helmets he was carry-ing. "There wasn't much to steal, I'm afraid—this submarine is not quite up to its former glory. Still, I found a small jewelry box hidden in the barracks, with a few valuable items."

"I think the ruby ring is very in," Esmé purred. "It would look wonderful with my flame-imitating dress."

"That was my mother's," Fiona said quietly.

"She would have wanted me to have it,"

Esmé said quickly. "We were close friends at
school."

"I want the necklace!" Carmelita demanded.
"It goes perfectly with my veterinarian stethoscope! Give it to me, Countie!"

"I wish we had those carnival freaks with
us," the hook-handed man said. "They could
help carry some of these uniforms."

"We'll see them at the Hotel Denouement,"
Count Olaf, "along with the rest of my comrades. Well, let's get out of here! We have lots
to do before we arrive! Triangle Eyes, take the
orphans to the brig! Ha ha hula dance!"

Humming a ridiculous tune, the villain performed a few dance steps of triumph, only to
stumble over the diving helmet on the floor.
Carmelita giggled nastily as Olaf reached down
and rubbed his tattooed ankle.

"Ha, ha Countie!" cried Carmelita. "My
dance recital was better than yours!"

"Get this hat out of here, Triangle Eyes,"
Count Olaf snarled. He bent down, picked up

the helmet, and started to hand it to Fiona, but the hook-handed man stopped him.

"I think you'll want that helmet for yourself, boss," the henchman said.

"I prefer a smaller, lighter hat," Count Olaf said, "but I appreciate the gesture."

"What my brother means," Fiona explained, "is that inside this helmet is the Medusoid Mycelium."

The Baudelaires gasped and looked at one another in horror, as Count Olaf peered through the helmet's tiny window, his eyes wide beneath his eybrow. "The Medusoid Mycelium," he murmured, and ran his tongue thoughtfully along his teeth. "Could it be?"

"Impossible," Esmé Squalor said. "That fungus was destroyed long ago."

"They brought it with them," the hook-handed man said. "That's why the baby was so sick."

"This is marvelous," Olaf said, his voice as raspy and wheezy as if he were poisoned himself.

"As soon as you Baudelaires are in the brig, I'm going to open this helmet and toss it inside! You'll suffer as I've always wanted you to suffer."

"That's not what we should do!" Fiona cried. "That's a very valuable specimen!"

Esmé stepped forward and draped two of her tentacles around Olaf's neck. "Triangle Eyes is right," she said. "You don't want to waste the fungus on the orphans. Besides, you need one of them alive to get the fortune."

"That's true," Olaf agreed, "but the idea of those orphans not being able to breathe is awfully attractive."

"But think of the fortunes we can steal!" Esmé said. "Think of the people we can boss around! With the Medusoid Mycelium in our grasp, who can stop us now?"

"No one!" Count Olaf cackled in triumph. "Ha Hunan chicken! Ha ha hamantaschen! Ha ha hors d'oeuvres! Ha ha h—"

But the Baudelaire children never learned what ridiculous word Olaf was going to utter, as he interrupted himself to point across the Main Hall at a screen on the wall. The screen looked like a piece of graph paper, lit up in green light, and at the center were both a glowing letter Q, representing the *Queequeg*, and a glowing eye, representing the terrible octopus submarine that had devoured them. But at the top of the screen was another shape—one they had almost forgotten about. It was a long curved tube, with a small circle at the end of it, slithering slowly down the screen like a snake, or an enormous question mark, or some terrible evil the children could not even imagine.

"What's that cakesniffing shape?" asked Carmelita Spats. "It looks like a big comma."

"Shh!" Count Olaf hissed, putting his filthy hand over Carmelita's mouth. "Silence, everyone!"

"We have to get out of here," Esmé murmured. "This octopus is no match for that thing."

"You're right," Olaf muttered. "Esmé, go whip our rowers so they'll go faster! Hooky, store those uniforms! Triangle Eyes, take the orphans to the brig!"

"What about me?" Carmelita asked. "I'm the cutest, so I should get to do something."

"I guess you'd better come with me," the count said wearily. "But no tap-dancing! We don't want to show up on their sonar!"

"Ta ta, cakesniffers!" Carmelita said, waving her pink wand at the three siblings.

"You're so stylish, darling," Esmé said. "It's like I always say: You can't be too rich or too in!"

The two wicked females jumped through the broken porthole and out of the *Queequeg*, followed by the hook-handed man, who gave the Baudelaires an awkward wave. But before Count Olaf exited, he paused, standing on the wooden table, and drew his long, sharp sword to point at the children. "Your luck is over at last," he said, in a terrible voice. "For far too long, you keep defeating my plans and escaping from my clutches—

a happy cycle for you orphans and an unprofitable one for me. But now the tables have turned, Baudelaires. You've finally run out of places to run. And as soon as we get away from *that*"—he pointed at the sonar screen with a flick of his sword, and raised his eyebrow menacingly—"you'll see that this cycle has finally been broken. You should have given up a long time ago, orphans. I triumphed the moment you lost your family."

"We didn't lose our family," Violet said. "Only our parents."

"You'll lose everything, orphans," Count Olaf replied. "Wait and see."

Without another word, he leaped out of the porthole and disappeared into his ghastly mechanical octopus, leaving the Baudelaires alone with Fiona.

"Are you going to take us to the brig?" Klaus asked.

"No," Fiona said. "Aye! I'll let you escape—if you can. You'd better hurry."

"I can set a course," Violet said, "and Klaus can read the tidal charts."

"Serve cake," Sunny said.

Fiona smiled, and looked around the Main Hall sadly. "Take good care of the *Queequeg*," she said. "I'll miss it. Aye!"

"I'll miss *you*," Klaus said. "Won't you come with us, Fiona? Now that Olaf has the Medusoid Mycelium, we'll need all the help we can get. Don't you want to finish the submarine's mission? We never found the sugar bowl. We never found your stepfather. We never even finished that code we were going to invent."

Fiona nodded sadly, and walked to the wooden table. She picked up *Mushroom Minutiae*, and then acted contrary to her personal philosophy, a phrase which here means "hesitated for a moment, and faced the middle Baudelaire." "When you think of me," she said quietly, "think of a food you love very much." She leaned forward, kissed Klaus gently on the mouth, and disappeared through the porthole

without so much as an "Aye!" The three Baudelaires listened to the mycologist's footsteps as
she joined Count Olaf and his comrades, and
left them behind.

"She's gone," Klaus said, as if he could hardly
believe it himself. He lifted one trembling hand
to his face, as if Fiona had given him a slap
instead of a kiss. "How could she leave?" he
asked. "She betrayed me. She betrayed all of us.
How could someone so wonderful do something
so terrible?"

"I guess her brother was right," Violet said,
putting her arm around her brother. "People
aren't either wicked or noble."

"Correctiona," Sunny said, which meant
"Fiona was right, too—we'd better hurry if we
want to escape from the *Carmelita* before Olaf
notices we're not in the brig."

"I'll set a course for Briny Beach," Violet
said.

Klaus took one last look at the porthole

where Fiona had disappeared, and nodded. "I'll look at the tidal charts," he said.

"Amnesi!" Sunny cried. She meant something along the lines of, "You're forgetting something!" and pointed one small finger at the circle of glass on the floor.

"Sunny's right," Klaus said. "We can't launch the submarine without repairing that porthole, or we'll drown."

But Violet was already halfway up the rope ladder that led to the *Queequeg*'s controls. "You'll have to repair that yourself, Sunny," she called down.

"Cook," Sunny replied. "Cook and teeth."

"We don't have time to argue," Klaus said grimly, pointing at the sonar screen. The question mark was inching closer and closer to the glowing Q.

"Aye," Sunny said, and hurried to the glass circle on the floor. It was still intact, but the youngest Baudelaire could think of nothing that could reattach the circle to the wall of the submarine.

"I think I've found the location device," Violet called down from the *Queequeg*'s controls. Quickly she flipped a switch, and waited impatiently as a screen came to life. "It looks like we're fourteen nautical miles southeast of the Gorgonian Grotto. Does that help?"

"Aye," Klaus said, running his finger over one of the charts. "We need to travel straight north to Briny Beach. It shouldn't be far. But how are we going to get out of the *Carmelita*?"

"I guess we'll just fire up the engines," Violet said, "and I'll try to steer us back through the tunnel."

"Have you ever steered a submarine before?" Klaus asked nervously.

"Of course not," Violet said. "We're in uncharted waters, aye?"

"Aye," Klaus said, and looked proudly up at his sister. The two Baudelaires could not help grinning for a moment before Violet pulled a large lever, and the familiar, whirring sound of the *Queequeg*'s engines filled the Main Hall.

"Gangway!" Sunny cried, squeezing past Klaus as she raced toward the kitchen. Violet and Klaus heard their sister fumbling around for a moment, and then the youngest Baudelaire returned, carrying two boxes the siblings recognized from their time in the town of Paltryville. "Gum!" she cried triumphantly, already ripping the wrappers off several pieces and sticking them into her mouth.

"Good idea, Sunny," Violet called. "The gum can act as an adhesive, and stick the porthole back together."

"That thing is getting closer," Klaus said, pointing to the sonar screen. "We'd better get the submarine moving. Sunny can do the repair work while we move through the tunnel."

"I'll need your help, Klaus," Violet said. "Stand at the porthole and let me know which way to turn. Aye?"

"Aye!" Klaus replied.

"Aye!" Sunny cried, her mouth full of gum. The elder Baudelaires remembered that their sibling had been too young for gum when the children were working at the lumbermill, and they could hardly believe she had grown up enough to be stuffing handfuls of the sticky substance into her mouth.

"Which way do I go?" Violet called from the controls.

Klaus peered out of the porthole. "Right!" he called back, and the *Queequeg* lurched to the right, traveling with difficulty in the little water at the bottom of the tunnel. There was an enormous scraping sound, and the Baudelaires heard a loud splashing from inside one of the pipes. "I mean, left!" Klaus said quickly. "You and I are facing opposite directions! Left!"

"Aye!" Violet cried, and the submarine lurched in the opposite direction. Through the porthole, the Baudelaires could see that they were moving away from the platform where Olaf had first greeted them. Sunny spat a huge wad of gum onto the glass circle, and spread it around with her hands on the circle's edge.

"Right!" Klaus cried, and Violet turned the *Queequeg* again, narrowly missing a turn in the passageway. The eldest Baudelaire looked nervously at the sonar screen, where the sinister shape was moving closer and closer to them.

"Left!" Klaus cried. "Left and down!" The submarine lurched and sank, and through the porthole the middle Baudelaire caught a brief glimpse of the rowing room, with Esmé holding the tagliatelle grande threateningly in one fake tentacle. Sunny hurriedly stuffed more gum into her mouth, moving her enormous teeth furiously to soften the candy.

"Left again!" Klaus cried. "And then a very sharp right when I say '*Now*'!"

"Now?" Violet called back.

"No," Klaus said, and held up one hand as Sunny spit more gum onto the glass circle. "*Now!*"

The submarine lurched violently to the right,

sending several objects tumbling from the wooden table. Sunny ducked to avoid being knocked on the head by the poetry of T. S. Eliot. "Sorry for the bumps," Violet called, from the top of the rope ladder. "I'm still getting the hang of these controls. What's next?"

Klaus peered out of the porthole. "Keep going straight," he said, "and we should exit the octopus."

"Help!" Sunny cried, spreading the rest of the gum on the edge of the circle. Klaus hurried to her side, and Violet raced down the rope ladder to help, leaving the submarine's controls alone so the *Queequeg* would travel in a straight line. Together, the three Baudelaires picked up the glass circle and climbed onto the wooden table so they could put the porthole back together.

"I hope it holds," Violet said.

"If it doesn't," Klaus said, "we'll know soon enough."

"On three," Sunny said, which meant something like, "After I say one and two." "One! Due!"

"*Three!*" the Baudelaire orphans said in unison, and pressed the glass circle against the hole Olaf had cut, smoothing the gum over the crack so that it might hold firm, just as the *Queequeg* tumbled out of the mechanical octopus into the chilly waters of the ocean. The Baudelaires pushed against the porthole together, their arms stretched out against the glass as if they were trying to keep someone from coming in a door. A few rivulets—a word which here means "tiny streams of water"—dripped through the gum, but Sunny hurriedly patted the sticky substance into place to stop the leaks. Her tiny hands smoothed the gum over the edge of the circle, making sure her handiwork was strong enough that the children wouldn't drown, but when she heard her siblings gasp she looked up from her work, looked through the repaired porthole, and stared in amazement at what she saw.

In the final analysis—a phrase which here means "after much thought, and some debate with my colleagues"—Captain Widdershins was wrong about a great many things. He was wrong about his personal philosophy, because there are plenty of times when one should hesitate. He was wrong about his wife's death, because as Fiona suspected, Mrs. Widdershins did not die in a manatee accident. He was wrong to call Phil "Cookie" when it is more polite to call someone by their proper name, and he was wrong to abandon the *Queequeg,* no matter what he heard from the woman who came to fetch him. Captain Widdershins was wrong to trust his stepson for so many years, and wrong to participate in the destruction of Anwhistle Aquatics, and he was wrong to insist, as he did so many years ago, that a story in *The Daily Punctilio* was completely true, and to show this article to so many volunteers, including the Baudelaire parents, the Snicket siblings, and the woman I happened to love. But Captain Widdershins was right about one thing. He was right to say that there are secrets in this world too terrible for young people to know, for the simple reason that there are secrets in this world too terrible for anyone to know, whether they are as young as Sunny Baudelaire or as old as Gregor Anwhistle— secrets so terrible that they ought to be kept secret, which is probably how the secrets became secrets in the first place, and one of those secrets is the long, strange shape the Baudelaire orphans saw, first on the *Queequeg*'s sonar, and then as they held the porthole in place and stared out into the waters of the sea. Night had fallen—Monday night—so the view outside was very dark, and the Baudelaires could scarcely see this enormous and sinister shape. They could not even tell, just as I will not tell, if it was some horrifying mechanical device, such as a submarine, or some ghastly creature of the sea. They merely saw an enormous shadow, curling and uncurling in the water, as if Count Olaf's one eyebrow had grown into an enormous beast that was roaming the sea, a shadow as chilling as the villain's glare and as dark as villainy itself. The Baudelaire orphans had never seen anything so utterly eerie, and they found themselves sitting still as statues, pressing against the porthole in an utter hush. It was probably this hush that saved them, for the sinister shape curled once more, and began to fade into the blackness of the water.

"Shh," Violet said, although no one had spoken. It was the gentle, low shushing one might do to comfort a baby, crying in the middle of the night over whatever tragedy keeps babies awake in their cribs, and keeps the other members of the baby's family standing vigil, a phrase which here means "keeping nearby, to make sure everyone is safe." It does not really mean anything, this shushing sound, and yet the younger Baudelaires did not ask their sister what she meant, and merely stood vigil with her, as the shape disappeared into the ocean of the night, and the children were safe once more. Without a word, Violet took her hands off the glass, climbed off the table, and resumed her place at the *Queequeg*'s controls. For the rest of their journey, none of the children spoke, as if the unearthly spell of that terrible secret shape were still lingering over them. All night long and into the morning, Violet worked the levers and switches of the submarine, to make sure it stayed on course, and Klaus marked their path on the charts, to make sure they were heading to the right place, and Sunny served slices of Violet's birthday cake to her fellow volunteers, but none of the three Baudelaires spoke until a gentle *bump!* rocked the *Queequeg*, and the submarine came to a gentle stop. Violet climbed down the rope ladder and ducked underneath a pipe to peer through the periscope, just as Captain Widdershins must have peered at the Baudelaires up in the Mortmain Mountains.

"We're here," she said, and the three Baudelaires left the Main Hall and walked down the leaky corridor to the room where they had first climbed aboard the submarine.

"Valve?" Sunny asked.

"We shouldn't have to activate the valve," Violet said. "When I looked through the periscope, I saw Briny Beach, so we can simply climb up the ladder—"

"And end up where we were," Klaus finished, "a long time ago."

Without any further discussion the Baudelaire children climbed up the ladder, their steps echoing down the narrow passageway, until they reached the hatch. Violet grabbed the handle to open it, and found that her siblings had each grabbed the handle, too, so all three children turned the handle together, and opened the hatch together, and together they climbed out of the passageway, down the outside of the submarine, and lowered themselves onto the sand of Briny Beach. It was morning—the same time of morning as the last time the Baudelaire children had been there, receiving the dreadful news about the fire, and it was just as gray and foggy as that terrible day. Violet even saw a slender, smooth stone on the sand, and picked it up, just as she had done so long ago, skipping rocks into the water without ever imagining she would soon be exploring its terrible depths. The siblings blinked in the morning sun, and felt as if some cycle were about to begin all over again—that once more they would receive terrible news, and that once more they would be taken to a new home, only to have villainy surround them once more, as had happened so many times since their last visit to Briny Beach, just as you might be wondering if the Baudelaires' miserable story will begin all over again for you, with my warning you that if you are looking for happy endings, you would be better off reading some other book. It is not a pleasant feeling, to imagine that the tables will never turn and that a tedious cycle will begin all over again, and it made the Baudelaires feel passive, just as they had in the waters of the Stricken

Stream, accepting what was happening without doing anything about it as they looked around at the unchanged shore.

"Gack!" Sunny said, which meant "Look at that mysterious figure emerging from the fog!" and the Baudelaires watched as a familiar shape stopped in front of them, took off a tall top hat, and coughed into a white handkerchief.

"Baudelaires!" Mr. Poe said, when he was done coughing. "Egad! I can't believe it! I can't believe you're here!"

"You?" Klaus asked, gazing at the banker in astonishment. "*You're* the one we're supposed to meet?"

"I guess so," Mr. Poe said, frowning and taking a crumpled piece of paper from his pocket. "I received a message saying that you'd be here at Briny Beach today."

"Who sent the message?" Klaus asked.

Mr. Poe coughed once more, and then shrugged his shoulders wearily. The children noticed that he looked quite a bit older than the last time they had seen him, and wondered how much older they looked themselves. "The message is signed J.S.," Mr. Poe said. "I assume that it's that reporter from *The Daily Punctilio*—Geraldine Julienne. How in the world did you get here? Where in the world have you been? I must admit, Baudelaires, I had given up all hope of ever finding you again! It was a shame to think that the Baudelaire fortune would just sit in the bank, gathering interest and dust! Well, never mind that now. You'd better come with me—my car's parked nearby. You have a great deal of explaining to do."

"No," Violet said.

"No?" Mr. Poe said in amazement, and coughed violently into his handkerchief. "Of course you do! You've been missing for a very long time, children! It was very inconsiderate of you to run away without telling me where you were, particularly when you've been accused of murder, arson, kidnapping, and some assorted misdemeanors! We're going to get right in my car, and I'll drive you to the police station, and—"

"No," Violet said again, and reached into the pocket of her uniform. She held up the telegram to her siblings and read:

"At the pink hour, when the eyes and back
  Turn upward from the desk, when the human engine waits
  Like a pony throbbing party . . .

"That's what's in the telegram." She paused, and scanned the horizon of the beach. Something caught her eye, and she gave her siblings a faint smile. "The real poem," she said, "goes like this:

"At the violet hour, when the eyes and back
  Turn upward from the desk, when the human engine waits
  Like a taxi throbbing waiting."

"Verse Fluctuation Declaration," Klaus said.

"Code," Sunny said.

"What are you talking about?" Mr. Poe demanded. "What is going on?"

"The missing words," Violet said to her siblings, as if the coughing banker had not spoken, "are '*violet*,' '*taxi*,' and '*waiting*.' We're not supposed to go with Mr. Poe. We're supposed to get into a taxi." She pointed across the beach, and the children could see, scarcely visible in the fog, a yellow car parked at a nearby curb. The Baudelaires nodded, and Violet turned to address the banker at last.

"We can't go with you," Violet said. "There's something else we need to do."

"Don't be absurd!" Mr. Poe sputtered. "I don't know where you've been, or how you got here, or why you're wearing a picture of Santa Claus on your shirts, but—"

"It's Herman Melville," Klaus said. "Goodbye, Mr. Poe."

"You are coming with me, young man!" Mr. Poe ordered.

"Sayonara," Sunny said, and the three Baudelaires walked quickly across the beach, leaving the banker coughing in astonishment.

"Wait!" he ordered, when he put his hand-kerchief away. "Come back here, Baudelaires! You're children! You're youngsters! You're orphans!"

Mr. Poe's voice grew fainter and fainter as the children made their way across the sand. "What do you think the word 'violet' means?" Klaus murmured to his sister. "The taxi isn't purple."

"More code," Sunny guessed.

"Maybe," Violet said. "Or maybe Quigley just wanted to write my name."

"Baudelaires!" Mr. Poe's voice was almost inaudible, as if the Baudelaires had only dreamed he was there on the beach.

"Do you think he's in the taxi, waiting for us?" Klaus asked.

"I hope so," Violet said, and broke into a run. Her siblings hurried behind her as she ran across the sand, her boots showering sand with each step. "Quigley," she said quietly, almost to herself, and then she said it louder. "Quigley! Quigley!"

At last the Baudelaires reached the taxi, but the windows of the car were tinted, a word which here means "darkened, so the children could not see who was inside." "Quigley?" Violet asked, and flung open the door, but the children's friend was not inside the taxi. In the driver's seat was a woman the Baudelaires had never seen before, dressed in a long, black coat buttoned up all the way to her chin. On her hands were a pair of white cotton gloves, and in her lap were two slim books, probably to keep her company while she waited. The woman looked startled when the door opened, but when she spied the children she nodded politely, and gave them a very slight smile, as if she were not a stranger at all—but also not a friend. The smile she gave them was one you might give to an associate, or another member of an organization to which you belong. "Hello, Baudelaires," she said, and gave the children a small wave. "Climb aboard."

The Baudelaires looked at one another cautiously. They knew, of course, that one should never get into the car of a stranger, but they also knew that such rules do not necessarily apply in taxis, when the driver is almost always a stranger. Besides, when the woman had lifted her hand to wave, the children had spied the name of the books she had been reading to pass the time. There were two books of verse: *The Walrus and the Carpenter, and Other Poems*, by Lewis Carroll, and *The Waste Land*, by T. S. Eliot. Perhaps if one of the books had been by Edgar Guest, the children might have turned around and run back to Mr. Poe, but it is rare in this world to find someone who appreciates good poetry, and the children allowed themselves to hesitate.

"Who are you?" Violet asked, finally.

The woman blinked, and then gave the

children her slight smile once more, as if she had expected the Baudelaires to answer the question themselves. "I'm Kit Snicket," she said, and the Baudelaire orphans climbed aboard, turning the tables of their lives and breaking their unfortunate cycle for the very first time.

LEMONY SNICKET

has received several citations for bravery in the face of evil and several more for caution when bravery might have proven to be more trouble than it was worth. He was last seen by witnesses who proved to be unreliable and/or of a particularly suspicious nature. In his spare time he hides all traces of his actions.

BRETT HELQUIST

was born in Ganado, Arizona, grew up in Orem, Utah, and now lives in Brooklyn, New York. In order to depict the tragic lives of the Baudelaire orphans, he uses broken pencils, dried-up paint, and boxes and boxes of tissues.

800 632

To My Kind Editor,

My enemies, I fear, are
with extremely long finge
so that you might never r

Lousy Lane ends in cul-de-
gas station attendant, wh
the complete manuscript,
anywhere near a match!

Remember, you are my last
be told to the general pu

With all due respect,

Lemony Snicket
Lemony Snicket

800

To My Kind

I must apolo
completely in
but I doubt i

Instead of dri
field of daisie
If you dig stra
book the **twelfth**

Remember, you are
be told to the g

With all due res

Lemony S.

Lemony Snicket

Hotel D

8   0   0   6

To My Kind Editor

I must once again
"third time's the
without anyone ri

The alleyway behind
an excellent hiding
the dreadful story
Do NOT USE THE ete

Remember, you are
be told to the genera

with all due respect,

Lemony Snicke

Lemony Snicket

Hot

8 0 0

To My Kind Edito

How many apologies
"fourth time's the
continued treachery

One of the curvies
a cup of very bitt
The twelfth book, e

Remember, you are my
be told to the general

With all due respect,

Lemony Snicket

Lemony Snicket

Hotel
8 0 0

To My Kind Editor,

Please accept yet
This time I am ce
impossible to des.

The Galway Kennel
barks the loudest,
chapter in his te

Remember, you are
be told to the gen

With all due respe

Lemony Snicket

Lemony Snicket

Hotel R
8 0 0

To My Kind Edi

The last saf
laundry of
title of th

Her name,

Remembe

With a